INNER SANCTUM MYSTERY

INNER SANCTUM MYSTERY   AN INNER SANCTUM

By the same author

an inner sanctum mystery

by **THOMAS WALSH**

THE TENTH POINT

simon and schuster · new york

¶ONE

THERE WAS NEVER even the least use, for either of the
two Ferguson sisters, in talking and talking about it;
and they each knew that. It was always the one agreed
fact of the matter, the part fully understood and accepted by each of them—no compromise. And yet night
after night that summer, despite the fact, and as soon as
Lucy had got home from the shop at six-thirty or seven,
they would resume talking about it almost at once, as if
somehow doggedly compelled to keep arguing the thing.
Perhaps each of them felt that it was necessary in order
to show the other that no concession was anywhere at all

in sight yet; and so Ellen Ferguson would sit clumsily at the table, face averted, eyes sulky and bitter, mouth set, although with the rather desperate feeling in her that she was fighting not only against her sister Lucy now, but against a great many other factors behind and supporting Lucy. Against the plainest of common sense, to admit that much; against the overwhelming knowledge of her complete material dependence these days; and also, worst of all, her own feelings of shame and guilt in what had happened. She had, therefore, no reasonable arguments with which to defend herself. She managed to defend, however. "No," she would say, as soon as the opportunity presented itself. "I won't. I won't do it, I tell you. I don't care."

"Well, I knew that," Lucy would say, nodding over at her with a forced assumption of calmness. "It's the way you've been acting all along, anyway. You really don't care, do you? So go ahead and break Aunt Eleanor's heart when she finds out about it—and she will sooner or later, remember. I can't always go on writing those letters back home about how happy you are up here, and what a wonderful job you've got. She'll find out the truth for herself one of these days, and so will everyone else, too. And of course you know how she'll feel, then. You'll have broken her heart, that's all. Her sweet little Ellie! But of course if that's what you want, after everything that she did for you . . . Is it? And don't keep sitting there with that look on your face as if—answer me. I just asked you a plain question. Did you hear?"

It was impossible not to hear. It was possible not to answer, however. So Lucy would get up, the forced calmness departing rapidly now, and smoke a cigarette in quick, furious puffs, her eyes glittering. She would walk over to the window and stare out. Perhaps a minute or two would drag by. And presently, coming back, she would begin all over again.

"Then don't answer me. It's not worth the trouble, I imagine. But who do you suppose is going to look out for it around here? Who'll have the time? Who'll have the chance to be home with it all day? And who's going to have the money, for that matter? I can't even scrape up enough rent for the shop some months, and you know that. You know it because I'm tired telling you; and yet you still seem to think that you can sit there and keep defying me. No. No, you won't. That's all you can say. You won't, you won't, you won't. Well, you will—or else I'll simply refuse to take the responsibility any more. You know how Aunt Eleanor worked to bring us up after Mamma died, and you know what something like this could do to her, the way she's feeling these days. And still, now that you've got to decide one way or the other about it . . ."

She would not be answered that time, either. There was nothing to answer, really—which was always the pattern of the thing, night after night after night. All the logic, all the hard, sensible practicality on Lucy's part; nothing but the sullen and despairing hopelessness on Ellen's. She had been eighteen years old that February. Lucy was twenty-six. Night after night after night. . . .

And then Lucy would try it with her once more, one last time. She would sit down at the table. She would light another cigarette. She would revert to the forced calmness again.

"And what's against it?" she would demand reasonably. "Can you explain that, even? You know in your heart that there are a lot of people in this world, and good, decent people, who really want children, and would do anything to get one. Think about that for a minute. What could they offer to it, do you suppose, and what can you offer? Well, speak up. Where would it have a comfortable home provided, and a father and

7

mother who loved and wanted it, and the kind of background it would never have to be ashamed of later on? It's the only thing to do, I tell you. You'll have to put it out for adoption somewhere. I don't care what you want, or what you don't want. You've got to do it, that's all. You've just got to!"

Which was nothing but plain common sense again, presented point after point to the sullenly averted face, the dry, stingingly hot eyes, the shamed, bitter mouth. May, June, July; the beginning of August. Have to, have to, have to. Good, decent people; Aunt Eleanor back home; have to, have to, have to. Why couldn't she understand?

But then in the end, although neither of them ever gave in by so much as a fraction of an inch to the other, the problem was made to settle itself, actually. The time drew near, and Lucy discovered a private nursing home in a sleepy little upstate village along the Hudson where no one would bother to investigate either of them, probably, and where Ellen could be passed off as an unfortunate young widow—a Mrs. John Franklin, perhaps. And that was just about the best answer all around, in Lucy's opinion. No one would have any idea who they were up there; no one would inquire about them; no one would gossip. And so, with the other question still bitter and unresolved between them, they did it in that way. They arrived at the nursing home on a breathlessly hot summer morning, the two of them; and the child, a little girl, was born about four o'clock the next afternoon, which was the afternoon of August 12, 1957.

It lived about eight hours. There was a Katie Stoner who ran the nursing home—a stout, smiling, hypocritically sweet woman—and a fumbling old doctor who smelled of cheap cigars and cheaper whiskey; and they told her about it the next morning, when the anesthesia

8

had worn off. A heart defect, Dr. Bennett explained. Everything had been done for it; but unfortunately, in such cases . . .

She asked one or two vague questions. Dr. Bennett answered them. After that she began to cry weakly. "Now, now," Dr. Bennett said, patting her hand by way of small comfort. Then he glanced around blearily, located his cigar butt on the edge of the dresser, picked it up, put it back in his mouth and motioned for Lucy and Katie Stoner to take over.

But it was all right. It seemed to Ellen that she felt nothing at all, deeply; that she had known what would happen—had known all along, by some instinct. Of course. It was the child nobody had wanted, not even the mother. She told Lucy about that, in what she felt was a calm and detached manner, and Lucy broke down suddenly and completely—cold, practical Lucy. She had to go out into the hall, and stay out there, with Katie Stoner to comfort her.

Three days went by. Then at last they permitted Ellen out of bed. But by that time everything had been taken care of, and there was nothing to do but visit a grave in the local cemetery with Lucy and the Stoner woman. One pathetic spray of wilted flowers was on the grave—Lucy's. They stood around. Presently the Stoner woman gave a deep, audible sigh, shaking her head, but with her round face and shiny black eyes detached as always from the expression of a truly genuine feeling. Even then it seemed to Ellen that she felt nothing of real consequence; or else, unadmitted, a shamed, secret relief that it was all over at last, with no problem any more, and no need to plan and contrive further. They got home about six to Lucy's apartment, a cheap, three-room walk-up in the East Bronx. It was raining a little by that time. They had something to eat.

"But now it's all over with," Lucy said, when they

were preparing for bed afterward. "And the thing you've got to do is to put it out of your head, Sis; just forget the whole business, that's all. And you can forget it if you make up your mind. You're still young enough, thank goodness. Look. I remember you used to talk about being a nurse back home, before all this happened to you. Well, why don't you think about it again? You still could, remember. Because nobody else ever has to know about this, nobody at all. So why not? Would you like me to write around in a day or two to some of the really good hospitals up here?"

A nurse? Ellen asked herself. The idea had no special attraction for her. She considered it listlessly, not seeming to care at the moment either way. She stirred after a while, still indifferent.

"I don't know," she said, feeling a new and rather childlike submission to Lucy, no more sullen stubbornness. "I haven't thought, really. Whatever you want, I suppose. Why not? I've got to support myself."

So they discussed it for a while; and the next evening, when Lucy got home about seven-thirty, they decided on it. The new life began after that. In September of that year, Ellen went into training and discovered that she did like it—as much as she would have liked anything else, probably. She persisted, in any event; and in her graduation picture on the hospital steps a stout, jolly-looking girl named Carol Proctor stood next to her. They had been close friends throughout training. They remained close. Some years later, and also in the month of August, oddly enough, Carol Proctor wrote her a long letter.

¶ TWO

IT'S SO MUCH out of this world," was the way Carol Proctor began describing the place, on the first of her five or six handwritten pages, "I mean it really is, sweetie, that I don't know how to begin telling you about it. But anyway. It's got everything that money can buy, believe me; a swimming pool and a tennis court and a riding ring and a big apple orchard out back, and a view from my bedroom window up on the third floor that makes me feel like I'm living in the middle of a big park all by myself, with none of you common people to worry about. And the food they serve you! Why, I'll

11

never be able to even look at that hospital slop when I get back. I've been spoiled sick. Fresh garden tomatoes big enough to stun a horse with; lamb kidneys sautéed for breakfast in sherry wine, if you like 'em that way, which I'm beginning to; and homemade muffins and pastry that I founder myself on every mealtime. I'm getting enormous!

"They call the place Ridge Hill, and I don't know how many rooms it has. I couldn't guess, even. But it's lovely. Nice yellowish old brick, with blue shutters, of course a real pale blue, and a lot of chimney stacks and tall, narrow windows, and a view over the river that will knock your eye out, and a formal garden, and beautiful old trees, and a lawn you could sleep in, it's that soft and deep, and an entrance hall that has an enormous arched window in back, and an oak stairway that's right out of one of those old Bette Davis society movies on the late show.

"I couldn't guess how many servants there are, either. Plenty, though. The housekeeper is a real sweet old thing named Mrs. Bradley, and of course there's a chauffeur and a cook and two cute little Scotch maids who live in, and some cleaning women and a few other peasants from the village for day help. There's a governess for the kid, too, a Miss Thornton, only the way she acts you'd think she belonged here by divine right or something, where common ordinary nurses like me and Tottie Chisholm ought to enter and leave by the back door. She's bloody high-toned British, you know— genuine clawss—or so she thinks. Chisholm and I call her Queen Gwendolyn.

"But anyway. What can she spoil? I'm going to drop her flat on her back one of these days, just for fun. You know me. What I'm writing about, though—Tottie Chisholm wants to go off the case next Monday. She's getting a little fed up with all the country air and quiet

12

around here; and then I think she's worried about that cute little Italian intern who was giving her a rush all spring. He hasn't written in two weeks now. So how about it? Like to take over for her?

"Because you could; no trouble at all. I guess you remember the son-in-law, Robert Burden, from the hospital last month, when you relieved me for those two days with Mrs. Cannaday. He remembers you, anyway, because when he was in the room with me yesterday afternoon he said why didn't I get someone up from New York to replace Tottie Chisholm, if I wanted to; maybe I could get someone like that nice, quiet Miss Ferguson. Well, of course I didn't know, I said—playing it real cute, see? Everybody was just crazy about Miss Ferguson, I told him. All the doctors liked her, and all her old patients wanted her back again. But I said I'd do what I could, naturally. I'd write and find out. So I'm writing, sweetie. And I'm also reminding you that his wife Monica died up here years ago, when the kid was born. Now that's a long time back, and maybe he's ripe for a little womanly comfort again. Of course it does seem to be the Cannaday money running this place, from the gossip I've heard; but still he's little Elizabeth's father, and I imagine he's going to be pretty well fixed when the old lady goes, because Monica was the one child she had, and there aren't any other relatives to cut in on the boodle. So it's worth a try, isn't it? A word to the wise, sweetie. He's kind of a cold fish; but maybe, if you're smart enough to work on him in the right way . . ."

The coffee began to perk. Setting the letter to one side, Ellen put some cold cereal into a bowl, and added sugar and milk. She had begun smiling faintly to herself. Page after page, in exuberant detail; so Carol Proctor must certainly want a little agreeable company up there, despite the physical attractions. But up where?

She reached for the envelope, turned it over and glanced at the postmark.

Even then it was rather difficult to make out. The lettering was a bit smudged. She moved over toward the kitchen window, for more light, and then made a quick, altogether instinctive gesture of recoil, dropping the envelope. She looked down at it, a bit shaken. Up there, she found herself thinking painfully—in that place. She picked up the envelope, went back to the table with it and heard Lucy begin to stir around in the bedroom passage. She glanced back over her shoulder quickly, then crumpled the envelope in one hand and thrust it well down under some other papers in the kitchen wastebasket.

But of course that was a very stupid reaction; no sense to it. She collected herself, sitting down once more at the kitchen table; and then, after the ugly and unexpected shock she had just received, went on with the letter.

"And I won't kid you about the patient," Proctor had written. "She isn't any better than she was last month, when we had her in the hospital down there after her second stroke; she's probably worse, I guess, because she had a pretty bad turn two weeks ago. Now she can just move one hand a little, and kind of mumble at you if she wants anything, but that's all. It's hard to understand her, too, unless you guess at it, and her mind wanders. She'll try to talk about people dead twenty years, and Chisholm says one night about two in the morning she wanted to see her lawyer. Then she just forgets the whole thing. I suppose it's what a head-shrinker would call free-floating anxiety. She just has to worry about something, whatever it is. But mostly she's quiet enough, though. A real nice old girl.

"And that's about it, sweetie, if you're even the least bit interested. But why don't you drive up some after-

14

noon this week, and see for yourself? You could just give me a ring first. There's a kind of dotty old gal from the local hospital up here on days, seven to three; I do three to eleven; and Tottie Chisholm, of course, is on nights.

"Now that would be your spot, if you decided to come. And I wish you would. But let me know right away, will you? We'll just have to arrange for somebody by next Monday. I do think we could have a regular ball here, the two of us. The whole countryside is just lovely now. Maybe you don't know what it's like up here. But once you've seen it . . ."

Again Ellen put down the letter. Over the years, whenever anything came up to draw her mind back to the Stoner nursing home, or to anyone connected with it, she had developed something in the nature of a conditioned reflex. The reflex was to divert her thoughts immediately to whatever offered; and now, the letter finished with, she attempted to divert them to Mrs. Cannaday.

But she had taken care of the woman for only two days last month, to relieve Proctor; so all she remembered from that brief period was gray hair, a tired and sunken gray face, a slow, thick articulation of speech when necessary—and that had even worsened by now, according to Proctor. She discovered, somewhat to her surprise, that the son-in-law was a bit more vivid to her.

Mr. Robert Burden . . .

She began to recall, without any marked favor, a tanned, fleshy face; a rather heavy physical build; sleepy brown eyes, a bit on the dull side; sandy brown hair; and an overall impression of self-indulgent physical sleekness and well-being. They had exchanged only a few words, when he came in to visit Mrs. Cannaday one Saturday afternoon; then two or three times they had smiled at one another in the hospital corridor. Yet he

15

had remembered her as that nice Miss Ferguson, if Proctor was correct; and how very gracious and condescending of him, that nice Miss Ferguson thought grimly. She had admired the type once, accepting the casual and outwardly agreeable indifference toward other people as true man-of-the-world polish; as perhaps it was. But once bitten, she thought grimly again, turned out to be twice shy. You could smell it on them, once you got past seventeen, anyway—the money, the position, the easy arrogance of expression and manner. It would be, for Mr. Robert Burden, exactly what it had been for that other someone seven years ago—the things he wanted, the full, satisfying life he was somehow entitled to. And if other people were silly and tiresome enough to expect anything else, to remember promises, for instance . . .

Lucy appeared, a tall, coolly graceful girl beautifully turned out in crisp green linen.

"A letter?" she inquired, pouring out the first cup of coffee for herself. "And a nice long one, too. Well—who's it from?"

Ellen told her.

"And she wants me to go up there next Monday and take over for Tottie Chisholm," she added reluctantly, while Lucy sat down on the other side of the table from her and began eating half a piece of dry toast. "But I don't know," she went on, still finding it painfully difficult, even with Lucy, to refer in any way to a dingy clapboard house at—at 214 Maple Avenue, was it?—"I can't seem to make up my mind about it. What do you think?"

"Well," Lucy said, not quite interested as yet, "it certainly sounds pretty nice, doesn't it? Why don't you? Up in Westchester, did you say?"

"Further than that," Ellen told her. She was a small, brown-haired girl, sturdily attractive in her own right, and with a rather marked air of personal independence about her; but there were moments when she had the helpless idea that she was never sturdy and independent at all, not when there were just she and Lucy talking together. She added reluctantly again: "It does. It sounds wonderful, of course. Only—well, it's up there, that's all; where you had to take me that time. You know. You remember the Stoner woman, don't you?"

"The who?" Lucy said, lifting her eyes slowly, in quite her usual composed manner. "What woman did you say? Who are you talking about?" But the Ferguson sisters had always quick and unerring emotional intuitions about one another; and so now, even before any further answer could be made, Lucy permitted herself a slow, thoughtful frown and put down her coffee cup.

"Oh," she said. "Well, I thought there was something else. You looked funny. So that's it."

"That's it," Ellen agreed. Her smile had become a bit forced; but then she had never been able to think of Katie Stoner, or of the house at 214 Maple Avenue, without a feeling of shamed, furtive guilt in her; without an idea, as it were, and against all the factual evidence, that the child nobody wanted had been quite deliberately abandoned seven years ago, because what had happened to it was what everybody concerned had wanted to happen, if they had only been honest enough to put the thought into plain words. The feeling was a little worse sometimes than at others. It was rather bad now. So she turned away from the table, feeling the guilt stir another slow, very ugly wriggle in her.

"That's it," she repeated. "Proctor makes it all sound like a vacation at Lake Placid. But I wonder if . . . Oh, well. What do you think?"

It was the second time she had asked that question in just a minute or two. It rather irritated her. But why was it necessary to be told this, and suggested that, when the only question was what she herself wanted to do?

17

Why should she be invariably so humble and submissive to Lucy? She was twenty-five years old now, after all. And so . . .

"I see," Lucy nodded. She tapped out a cigarette on the table, took more thought for a moment and pronounced judgment. "Well," she said, "if you want my opinion, I wouldn't go near the place. You'd only upset yourself. You'd be a fool. It wouldn't be worth it, Ellie. But, look here. We might plan something for this weekend, just the two of us. How would that be? We could take a little trip somewhere; perhaps up to Cape Cod. Eileen Fagin invited us, and you like her. So how about it?"

She was still beautifully poised, glancing over the newspaper headlines at the same time; but she had forgotten something. She had forgotten that if she could catch certain emotions and undercurrents in Ellen, there was a reciprocal law by which Ellen, and just as intuitively, was able to catch them in her.

So Ellen did not answer immediately. Instead, opening the dishwasher in their smart little red-and-white kitchen, she inserted a dish or two. But she had understood at once, despite Lucy's airy nonchalance, that Lucy did not want her to even consider taking that job up at Ridge Hill; and that, in addition, the idea of a few days up at Cape Cod had been deliberately suggested just now in order to turn her mind from it. Lucy did not take casual weekends, even in summer. There was the shop. But why should Lucy attempt to manage her in this way? Simple sisterly concern, was it—or something else?

Something else?

She closed the dishwasher. Perhaps it was only the time of year, she reflected miserably; August was always a very bad month for her. But here she was, at any rate, imputing hidden and mysterious motives to Lucy all of

18

a sudden, when it was Lucy who had done everything in the world for her seven years ago. And since, too. Even Proctor had been a bit overawed by the kind of sister that Lucy Ferguson was. "Why, she's one in a million," Proctor had remarked wistfully no more than a few weeks ago. "Look how she dresses you from her shop, sweetie; anything you want. And then look at that swell apartment where she lets you live for nothing at all, practically. What kind of a secret hold do you have on her, anyway? She's always buying you something. You just don't know how lucky you are."

A secret hold . . . Altogether absurd, of course. It was just that there were no money troubles at all now, not with Lucy Ferguson Gowns having been built up into a smart and successful Madison Avenue shop over the years; but certainly there had been plenty of money troubles that other time. And still Lucy had shouldered through, somehow. She had managed the thing. What would have happened, otherwise? Only . . . only what?

But she did not know that. She did not have even the faintest idea of what was troubling her. The child, perhaps? But surely, if the uneasy idea came every so often that the child had been failed in some manner, that it had not been wanted enough—or wanted at all, really—and that what had happened to it had been accepted with shameful and despicable relief, none of that could be put down to Lucy's fault, not with any fairness at all. She should, rather, be deeply grateful to Lucy; and she was. Only . . . The only again! She set her teeth. A touch of the old stubbornness roused in her. She turned slowly around from the dishwasher to face Lucy.

"You know," she said, without realizing immediately that something in her had decided a very personal problem for the first time in quite a while, and without regard for whatever Lucy might think of it, "you know I

19

might drive up there tomorrow, anyway—just to see. I don't know why I should get so awfully upset about it. I'm not that silly and emotional, am I?"

"Drive up where?" Lucy said. But she must certainly have understood where. They had just been talking about it. She decided to remember, in any event. She poured a little more coffee for herself, mouth compressed.

"Then do what you want," she said coldly. "Take the car. But I hope you realize what you'll be starting up for yourself. You know the sensible thing to do—to push it out of your mind once and for all. Then why don't you? What's the matter, anyway?"

"I wish I knew," Ellen admitted, still miserable. "I'm sorry."

"Brooding yourself sick about it," Lucy said. She was distinctly annoyed now. Her lips curled. "Year after year. When anyone with good sense—"

"Or else running and running from it," Ellen put in, perhaps not quite so evenly as she wanted. "What's the difference? It's the same thing either way, isn't it?"

"If you let it be," Lucy snapped, irritably throwing the newspaper to one side. "But I don't know why I bother talking to you. You just won't listen to anyone, and you never would. How many times has Tony Quinlan called you up this past month? And yet the way you treat that man . . . Oh, you make me sick and tired, sometimes. Go on up to that place tomorrow, if you've made up that so-called mind of yours. Do whatever you want to do. Torment yourself like a fool. You will, anyway. And who cares any more?"

She marched out angrily, whipping up her hat and purse in the apartment foyer, and then slamming the hall door to further express herself. Ellen remained out in the kitchen, still smiling painfully. But perhaps Lucy was right. Perhaps she was still running from 214

20

Maple Avenue; and as a result, for precisely the same reason, running and running from Tony Quinlan. Was that possible at all? It might have been. Twice that morning, at any rate, the phone rang on and on patiently. And twice, simply because it might have been Tony Quinlan, she refused to answer it.

¶THREE

Bᴜᴛ sʜᴇ ᴅʀᴏᴠᴇ up to Ridge Hill the next morning, finding herself as mule-stubborn about that part—and for what reason?—as Lucy had predicted. She started off in the car about nine thirty, and was able to turn off the parkway at a few minutes past twelve.

The local cemetery was a bit south of town. She stopped off there, with a two-dollar potted plant from one of the roadside stands, as if to prove to herself that the child was not quite forgotten by anyone; not coldly and callously abandoned in that other August of seven years gone. Abandoned, however? It seemed rather odd how that particular verb presented itself time after time. And no excuse for it, either; not even a shadow of excuse. Well . . .

Over near the far corner, she remembered; a quiet corner. There was a headstone there now with the name Franklin on it, which was the name Lucy had chosen for her at Katie Stoner's; a small, plain headstone which she had bought several years ago, without Lucy's knowledge. She stayed perhaps five minutes. Then she got back into the car, feeling a bit cold and empty inside, and called Proctor from the next gas station. A headstone without even the right name on it; a two-dollar potted plant; a child nobody had ever wanted . . . Proctor came on.

"So where are you?" Proctor demanded. "At what gas station? Okay. Turn left on Greenway Road, along the river, and then go straight on until you come to the third driveway down. It's got a stone wall on each side, and a cute little red-and-white sign that says Ridge Hill. You can't miss it, sweetie; say five minutes. I'll be out front waiting for you."

And she did not miss it. There was a gravel drive, summer-drowsy in a design of patched sunlight and shadow, and presently she could see the house beyond, and a plump figure waving to her from a gravel turnaround. On each side of the terrace steps were oversized stone urns with red and white flowers bobbing in them, and on her right the majestically calm surface of the Hudson—a dark, clean blue, just slightly ruffled, flashing at her across a near background of open and sunny meadows, and a far one of pleasantly wooded low hills. Proctor ran forward, still waving exuberantly. She drove in on the turnaround, parked well over to one side of it and got out.

It had been oppressively hot in the city, even at nine thirty in the morning. Here, on almost the stroke of

23

high noon, it was a beautifully clear summer day. And Proctor had not exaggerated anything at all; she had scarcely done full justice, incredibly enough. There was the house now, three stories high, built of warm, mellow old brick, but still looking long and low, comfortably settled in place; a row of French windows to each side of the front door; and tall, narrow shutters of delicate pale blue lying back beside them. In one quick glimpse she saw the swimming pool off to her right, with a red barn behind it, and a small riding ring; the apple orchard in back, on a low rise; and two big, sad-looking Dalmatians who were padding down silently from the terrace, after Proctor, in order to keep an eye on things. Only a few immaculate puffs of white cloud drifted across the sky, and under them the whole countryside was etched out in crystal-sharp focus—the rich, open green of lawn and meadow, the darker and more varied green of the woods flanking them. The air was good country air, cleanly fragrant, and over everything there was a pleasant feeling of things ordered, and well ordered; of calm serenity. She and Proctor greeted one another.

"Well, what did I tell you?" Proctor demanded, glancing around smugly, as if the first general effect up here was due to extremely cunning personal management on her part. "Did I lie to you, sweetie? Did I? But don't stand there like a hillbilly in her bare feet. The gentry might see you like that. Come on. Let me show you inside now."

They crossed the terrace, with the Dalmatians again padding along behind them. There was a fieldstone fireplace in the big reception hall; a red-and-black Chinese rug before the fireplace; a bowl of flowers under the beautiful curved stairway that Proctor had mentioned; and more flowers, in matching floor vases of almost translucent jade porcelain, at each side of the fireplace. Sunlight streamed down through the big arched window

24

in back, not a speck of dust visible in it anywhere; and a little maid in a gray uniform dress and white apron smiled shyly at them from the doorway of what might have been the kitchen passage in back.

"So what do you think?" Proctor demanded once more. "Not bad for a modest little country hideaway, is it? All you'd need would be twenty or thirty million dollars to keep it up, sweetie. Now I can give you the extra special, ten-dollar tour of the whole joint, or I can take you upstairs and let you freshen up a bit. What'll it be? It's almost lunch time."

"Upstairs," Ellen told her, a bit awed, and not quite sure whether or not she was going to trip on something, or break something. "Oh, Proctor! It's just lovely."

"And even an elevator," Proctor said, grandly leading the way to that, also. "So hop in, sweetie. What time did you leave?"

They rode up in the elevator, and on the third floor turned left to Proctor's bedroom—a square, comfortable chamber on the south side of the house, with a view out over the woods on that side, and over the riding ring with the freshly painted white fence around it.

"Now the first thing," Proctor said, after comfortably sprawling on the big bed. "You're going to take the case, aren't you? I'm counting on it."

"Well, I'm not sure," Ellen said, again hesitating a moment. "I might. How's Mrs. Cannaday?"

"Not too good," Proctor admitted reluctantly. "Not lately. We just keep her as comfortable as we can, and that's all. She kind of lost heart this past week or two, Dr. McCormick thinks. Poor old girl. She's been sick a year and a half, of course, and she knows we aren't helping her very much. She lies there and cries like a kid sometimes. It really gets you."

"I suppose," Ellen agreed soberly. "Yes, it would. What does Dr. McCormick think?"

25

"You tell me," Proctor said. "She has a lot of cardiac damage now to go with the blood pressure; and then she just doesn't seem to fight any more. But you can't ever be sure about them. She might conk out five minutes from now, if something happened, and she might keep going for the next couple of months, maybe. I'll take you down to say hello to her later on, when I relieve Ethel Cotter. But what time is it? One o'clock yet?"

It was five of. She bounced up.

"Then go in there and wash your ears," she directed. "And real good, too. But don't wake Tottie Chisholm; she's right next door here, and she never gets up till three or four in the afternoon. You sure about all your forks, sweetie? There'll be a couple of uniformed footmen serving you off the gold plate downstairs, and I think they'll be watching you."

"Oh, shut up," Ellen said. She was beginning to feel a great deal better, however; Carol Proctor was always an effective tonic for her. But she went in and washed; and then they had lunch downstairs not in the big formal dining room which Proctor insisted on exhibiting to her, but in a smaller and sunnier one looking out over the kitchen garden.

Miss Cotter came in just as they were sitting down. She was the seven-to-three nurse, Ellen remembered, who commuted from town; a brisk but vaguely erratic little woman in the late fifties, wearing a frilly but not quite immaculate uniform, and with a curious habit of jerking her head every so often even when she wasn't talking to anyone, or apparently listening to anyone.

"Just ourselves," Proctor said, so innocent and demure about it that Ellen gave her a quick glance. "And isn't that nice? But it's Mrs. Bradley's day off, Fergy, and I think the kid and Queen Gwendolyn went shopping in Rhinebeck. And Massa Robert is playing golf, of course. There's a big country club in toward town a piece. He really has a life of it, all right. Didn't he ever work at any kind of a job, Miss Cotter?"

"Oh, don't even use the expression," Miss Cotter advised, primly fussing around with her old-fashioned pince-nez. "A job, indeed—and Mr. Robert Burden? Why, he's above anything like that, girl; far above. When he married into the family, of course, he was given some kind of courtesy title down at Cannaday Mills in South Carolina; a director or something. But I don't know if anybody could tell you what he directs, actually—unless it's where they can send his fine fat salary every month. They were all like that; all the Burdens. Oh, yes. Lords of the manor. The old father without a penny to his name, and the brother who shot himself. A bit touched, you know; bad blood somewhere. I'm just warning you about the kind that he is, girl."

"Oh?" Proctor said. She gave Ellen a slight nudge under the table, to indicate that there might be something rather good coming up now. "Is that right? Why, I thought the Burdens were one of the real fine old families up in this neck of the woods. I thought they had even more money than the Cannadays."

"Then you thought wrong," Miss Cotter said. This time she adjusted one of her cuffs, jerked her head again and smiled knowingly. "I could tell you about the fine old family they were. Oh, couldn't I! Because they had to lock up the mother for three years before she died—and I know that myself. I helped to take care of her. And the father, old Harry Burden—well, don't ask me. That's all. Young girls, you know; innocent young girls. That was his style. And where was it that young Roger shot himself, that time he got kicked out of college for something or other? Can you imagine? Or do you happen to know what a hussy house is, either of you?"

"A what?" Proctor said, also whispering. "Oh, no! Oh, Miss Cotter! You don't mean—"

"But I do," Miss Cotter said, adjusting the other cuff and then nodding complacently. "Oh, yes! And don't tell me, thank you. There's no need. But look at it yourself. They were all the same, father and sons. Why do you suppose your grand Master Robert married a poor delicate little thing like Monica Cannaday? Not for her looks, I can tell you. She never had any. But for—"

She glanced cautiously around, at the passage. Then, with another knowing gesture of sly, crafty significance, she extended her right hand toward them, and rubbed the thumb over the first two fingers quickly and greedily.

It must all have been amusingly familiar to Proctor, after several weeks of it. But for Ellen, who had already formed her own personal impression of Robert Burden, there was a certain fascination to what Miss Cotter had just said. She glanced at Proctor, and then over at the other woman.

"You mean for the money?" she asked uncertainly. "Is that it? But then why didn't Mrs. Cannaday do something?"

"Ask me no questions," Miss Cotter said, nodding primly again, "and I'll tell you no lies. But they were distant cousins, you know, the old lady and Harry Burden; and she always had a great fancy for young Robert. No sons of her own, unfortunately. That's how it was. And I suppose she wanted the family to go on, as they all do, with the money kept nice and tight in it. So—"

"So you didn't have to tell her anything about that, either," Proctor began giggling, as soon as they had been left alone once more. "Because she just knew, see? And I bet she does, sweetie. I bet she's got a nice private little barrel of dirt about everyone in this town. The Town Crier, isn't she? I thought you might get a kick out of her."

28

"I'm ashamed to say that I did," Ellen confessed. "There's a curious fascination to gossip like that. Do you think she knows what she's talking about?"

"I suppose in a way," Proctor said. "Maybe twisted a little. But it's too bad the kid isn't here today. You'd like her, Fergy. She had a birthday a while ago, and Dada bought her a black-and-white pony she's just crazy about. There it is now. Real sporty of the old boy, wasn't it?"

"Very nice," Ellen agreed. They had settled down on two redwood settees at one end of the swimming pool, and she found her thoughts drifting back to another child who would have had a birthday some time ago, if she had lived, of course. August 12th . . . A black-and-white pony for one; a headstone, a two-dollar potted plant for the other. She lay quietly in the warm afternoon sunlight, with Proctor chattering away. Then three o'clock came. Proctor changed into uniform up in her room. They came downstairs again and found Miss Cotter waiting for them in the second-floor corridor.

"How is she?" Proctor asked. "Any better this afternoon?"

"Oh, fretful," said Miss Cotter. "There's just nothing to please her today; nothing at all. And of course crying again."

They entered the room, a big, pleasant room all white and gold in the French manner. Mrs. Cannaday was lying on her left side in the bed, and so facing them. In good health she must have been a heavy and rather imposing woman, with strong features and a calmly sensible firm mouth. Now, however, her face had a gray, bloated look, saggy with loose flesh; her mouth had that sad, telltale twist to one side; her left eyelid, showing only a narrow streak of white under the lashes, hung down clumsily. She gave no sign that she was aware of either of them. A few heavy tears remained on her face.

29

She was whining to herself, with the obviously befuddled self-pity of the hopelessly ill, in a low, childish manner.

"Now what's this?" Proctor demanded, at once bustling around with professional briskness and authority. "What's the matter? Here, here. And just when I've brought Miss Ferguson in to say hello for a minute? We'll wash your face first, and then get you some nice cold orange juice. You remember Miss Ferguson, don't you?"

But there was no sign that Mrs. Cannaday did remember. The self-pity absorbed her. She managed to turn her head listlessly, the tears still shining, after which she made a very slight upward motion of her good hand. It was less difficult for her than an attempt at speech, probably. Proctor washed her face and hands, still scolding, and got her to drink a little of the orange juice through a glass straw. But almost at once she moved her hand feebly and petulantly again, to indicate enough, and they moved over to the other end of the bedroom, where there was a French writing desk between two of the windows.

"Now you see what I mean," Proctor murmured. "She's really lost a lot of ground since we had her in the hospital last month, hasn't she? But you ought to get along with her okay, though. You did before."

"I hope I will," Ellen said.

"Well, you will," said Proctor, adjusting the window shades against the late afternoon sunlight, and then walking back to the hall door with her. "Don't worry about it. We'll see you next Monday, then?"

"Next Monday," Ellen agreed, after only a very brief hesitation this time. "All right."

She glanced back at the room. The white wood paneling had a touch of gold in it here and there; the three windows in front looked directly west over the river;

there was a built-in bookcase on the left, a fireplace with a mirror over it, and the door to the bathroom. On the bedside table, behind jars and bottles, was the framed snapshot of a dark-haired little girl, dressed in riding clothes, who was standing beside the black-and-white pony that Ellen had glimpsed earlier.

"The kid," Proctor murmured to her. "And don't you ever move it away from there, Fergy; the old lady gets just frantic if that happens. So leave it right where it is, no matter what. You know how to get back on the parkway now?"

"I think so," Ellen said. She was still looking at the snapshot. It seemed a little familiar to her; perhaps she had seen Elizabeth at the hospital last month. Had she? She could not remember.

"And how's our Dr. Quinlan?" Proctor said, nudging her with a kind of spinsterish coyness. "You're still seeing him these days, aren't you?"

"Oh, yes," Ellen said; not quite truthfully, however. Tony . . .

"Well, you'd better," Proctor said. "I think he's worth it. And take it nice and easy on the ride home, will you? You look a little tired to me."

"Yes," Ellen said, smiling back effortfully. "I will."

It was still a fine August afternoon outside. When she got into the car, Proctor waved down at her from one of the bedroom windows, and she waved back. But she still had that disturbing heaviness in her; the child, Tony, 214 Maple Avenue—everything piling up inside again, and still no answer to any of it. There was very little afternoon traffic, thankfully. She stopped once for gas and a cold drink; and then at a quarter of six, just as she had closed the apartment door behind her, heard Lucy talking to someone on the living-room telephone.

"Well, ask her yourself," Lucy said. "Here she is right now, Tony." She glanced back at the foyer, pretending not to see Ellen's frantically denying gesture. "And come over for dinner Saturday night," she added blandly. "Then you can take her sporting somewhere. Oh, no trouble at all. No, really. Just hamburg or something. We'll be looking for you around six thirty, then. Here she is."

And she handed over the phone, having settled the whole business by that time. So there was nothing for Ellen to do but talk to him, and say that it would be just fine for Saturday. But again the truth was much different. It was not fine. Even Proctor had never been told about 214 Maple Avenue. Then how, possibly, could Tony Quinlan? It was that final and that miserably hopeless to her. And no way out, of course. Well . . . She ate something or other, and went to bed early after telling Lucy that she had got a bad headache on the ride down. She did not sleep, however. About two in the morning, giving up even the attempt, she got up quietly, Lucy puffing away in the other bed, and drank a glass of milk in the kitchen.

The child; 214 Maple Avenue; Tony . . . All the surrounding windows were dark; cars squatted bumper to bumper on the street downstairs, but no people were visible. She lit one of Lucy's cigarettes. The child . . . But suppose the child had lived seven years ago? Would she feel better or worse now? If only she had wanted it a little more! If only she could feel now that . . . She put out the cigarette, not really caring for it. Then all at once, in the way of such things, it came to her why that framed snapshot in Mrs. Cannaday's bedroom had seemed so very familiar a few hours ago.

She hesitated a moment, but the idea still persisted stubbornly. Then all right, she decided, feeling only a tired disgust at herself. Prove it. See just how stupid it was. So she went out to the foyer and turned on a small lamp there. After that it took her only a moment to grope back on the closet shelf for what she wanted, and to pull it down—a large cardboard box packed to the brim with a collection of old family snapshots, all of them jumbled together without sequence.

She sat down with the box. There were pictures of her mother and father, dead many years now; of her Aunt Eleanor back home, who had raised the two Ferguson girls; of Lucy; and of herself. At last, way down in the box, there was the snapshot she had been looking for through all the others.

She held it up under the lamp. It showed Ellen Margaret Ferguson when she had been six or seven years old, standing proudly beside a big, patient brown horse at her Uncle Carl's farm in Pennsylvania; Ellen Margaret Ferguson facing the camera in the same physical pose, and with just about the same expression on her face, as little Elizabeth Burden in that other snapshot.

She put it down after a time, the hushed stillness of half past two in the morning deepening around her, and discovered that she was cold, shaky and a bit frightened. But why frightened? There were just two little girls of the same age who had been caught quite by accident in the same physical posture, only with a black-and-white pony in one picture and Uncle Carl's patient Old Doc in the other. To be frightened by something like that was altogether absurd. But then, of course, there had been sick fancies in her all day; the dead child, the living child. Until finally . . .

She closed the box, put it back on the closet shelf and returned to bed. But why had she insisted on going up there today—to that place? Why had she deliberately stirred up the whole thing all over again? She needed a first-class psychiatrist, perhaps; someone who could explain quite calmly and clearly why she was still punishing herself in this manner. Lucy had been perfectly correct about it. Lucy had known right away what was going to happen—and it had happened. It was the pure insanity again, the idea that the Stoner woman and drunken old Dr. Bennett had lied to her, that the baby was not dead; the appalling idea that something much worse might have happened to it—that it might be lonely and miserable and even physically abused somewhere. The child nobody had wanted; nobody. Not even the mother . . .

She had discovered that there was a certain very definite point at which to stop thoughts of that kind. She could not always stop them, however. So now she turned hurriedly from the other bed in the room, from Lucy; she put her face into the pillow, and folded it back over herself. It was not the first time she had done that, or perhaps the twentieth; but it was the first time in years and years. She was fairly quiet, though. After everything had spent itself she got up again and smoked another cigarette in the living room.

And now what? She had a choice. She could be either stupid or intelligent about this thing, and of course the intelligent decision would be to call Proctor tomorrow morning and ask them to get another nurse up there at Ridge Hill. To run from it again—in other words, to keep it penned up in herself—and from now on never to stop running. That was the intelligent thing. And the stupid . . . She put out the cigarette, slowly, rather clumsily, and lit another. She was still huddled up in the living room at five in the morning. At one moment her mind was made up, to call Proctor; at the next moment it wasn't. It was like that on the Thursday, too, and on Friday. Then Saturday night came, and Tony Quinlan.

But it wasn't hamburg for Dr. Quinlan, not with Lucy in charge of everything. It was sidecar cocktails, rather, a two-inch shell steak and lemon pie; so that part of the evening went off beautifully. Afterward he and Ellen went to the musical comedy he had tickets for, and had a drink somewhere, and danced a bit. It did not seem to be of very much use, however, any of it; and Dr. Quinlan appeared to be quite aware of the fact when they walked into her apartment vestibule about two in the morning. She had just opened the inside door with her key. He stood back against the wall on his side, looking down in a rather expressionless way at the tip of his right shoe, and spinning his hat on one finger. He had a sharp, somewhat impatient manner, never suffering fools gladly, a little too much nervous energy in the way he handled himself, and very sharply intelligent black eyes.

"Now wait a minute," he said, finally stirring himself. "Just don't break your neck hustling over to that elevator, Ferguson. You mind if I ask you something?"

She smiled brightly. It seemed to her that she had been smiling brightly all night, whenever the occasion demanded it.

"Well, I don't know," she said. "What would you ask me?"

"Where you go," Tony Quinlan grunted. "Where you get yourself off to every time we go out together. That's what. Your sister Lucy fixed up this whole thing tonight. You didn't. So what is it, Ferguson? What's on your mind? The feeling I'm beginning to get is that you didn't want to go out at all; not with me. Anything to it?"

It was a direct and explicit question. It seemed to require a direct and explicit answer. She walked over to the elevator, trying to find the answer, and pressed the button. But there was a much quicker and easier way to finish it off now than by protesting to him; there was a way to do it with just two words, it came to her. She spoke the words.

"I'm sorry," she said. "I'm sorry, Tony."

"I wonder are you," he said. He was still not satisfied,

apparently. The black eyes were studying and appraising her. "I just wonder, Ferguson. There's something a little funny about you lately. I know when a girl likes me. I know when she doesn't, too. But now you just want to leave it like that. Prognosis negative, eh? Come off it, will you? What's the trouble?"

"Just a plain clinical report," she said, trying bright ness again. "And there ought to be one somewhere around, doctor. Is that it?"

"Don't get smart," Tony Quinlan advised softly, the eyes a bit darker now, and much more dangerous. "That isn't your style, Ferguson; and I don't like it. But what I did like, before you put up the Berlin wall, I liked a hell of a lot, if you're interested particularly. So what happened? I want to know. Has anybody been talking to you about me and that little supervisor up in Maternity?"

She managed to smile quite naturally that time. There was a queer humor somewhere.

"You mean Miss Naughton?" she said.

"I mean Willing Lucille," Tony Quinlan growled, looking almost savagely disgusted now. "Because that's what got your back up, isn't it? All right. All right, Ferguson. I admit it. She's been out with everybody on the staff, even old Walter Henry. So if you got the idea that it was anything grand and wonderful . . . Look here. That was way back, damn it; before I knew you. It was something that happened, that's all; and something that's never going to happen again, believe me. Don't act like an old maid schoolteacher about it. Grow up, will you?"

The humor was getting a little twisted now. She was in the elevator. She pressed her floor button.

"I didn't know that," she said. "That I struck you like an old maid schoolteacher. I never suspected it."

Then she did another very stupid thing. She flushed

36

darkly and helplessly, and he saw it. He did not understand what it indicated, however. He became even more
anxious.

"Well, I thought somebody told you," he growled
back, still savagely hangdog. "I thought that was it. And
if it was, I thought maybe we could discuss it intelli-
gently. You're the kind that builds up something like
that, Ferguson. You're not fooling anyone."

"Am I?" she said. "Oh. I didn't know, Tony." But
there was a rather numb thought in her about honest
confession. Now it should have been the same thing either way between them—the same act, at any rate; and
yet it wasn't. Her eyes stung her a bit; under good control, however. She pressed the button again.

"Please," she said. "I'm very tired, Tony. It's past
two."

"I don't care about that," he said, the Quinlan jaw
setting itself. "We got something to settle right now,
Ferguson. I'm not a character in a book; and so I don't
intend to walk back to a crummy hotel in the rain,
remember, feeling sorry as hell for myself. That just
didn't mean anything. But if you think I'm going to get
down on my knees every time you throw it at me . . .
That's what you want, isn't it? Admit it!"

"What I want . . ." she said, the humor bubbling
up a little perilously once more. "Well, I just couldn't
say, I suppose. So there isn't much use to try, is there?"

"Guess there isn't," he said, wetting his lips delicately.
"Okay. You're the girl from the Frozen North, all right;
the one and original. They warned me. But I'll tell you
something. You can answer your phone tomorrow. It's
going to be all right from now on; no more Tony Quinlan. I give you my word, Ferguson. So you get what you
want; you get only the best. You get the kind of damned
fool that never even kissed a girl in his whole life—and
then see how you like it. Happy days, eh?"

37

He seemed to be in a cold rage by this time. He stood back; the elevator door slid shut; and that was the way it all ended between them that Saturday night—if it had ever begun, actually. That was the way she stopped running at last from Tony Quinlan.

But there was another effect. For some rather obscure reason, it helped her to stop running away from the other thing. She had her mind all made up about that the next morning. Lucy argued with her. Lucy lost her temper, even. It did no good. The old stubbornness was back in her. She packed Sunday afternoon, one big bag and one small one; and on the Monday morning, without hearing a word from Tony Quinlan again, just as promised, she boarded a slow, midmorning local from Grand Central Station.

¶FOUR

THE RIDE UP took about three hours. She read her paper; she glanced out at the river every once in a while; she dozed briefly. At twenty minutes past one, she got off the train, and discovered that she would have to share a taxicab with two other passengers. They had destinations in town. They were dropped first. And one of them, a nice-looking young boy in a spick-and-span Marine uniform, was dropped on the other side of the street from 214 Maple Avenue.

But the Stoner nursing home was no longer as dingy and unkempt as she had remembered it. A late-model sedan stood in the driveway; the lawn was mowed, and the hedge trimmed neatly along the walk; there were new aluminum screens, and fresh white curtains behind them. Every detail now, in sharp contrast to seven years ago, indicated a solid middle-class prosperity these days for Katie Stoner. Or had the house been sold in the meantime? She could have asked the driver about that. She did not. So it appeared that the new stubbornness in her, the decision to stop running at long last, had certain rather marked boundaries.

They rode out to Ridge Hill. And there, of course, for the first hour or two, there was the rather pleasant bustle of settling herself in. She met the housekeeper, Mrs. Bradley, a stout, friendly woman; she unpacked her uniforms, with Proctor helping; and she had a quick shower for herself to get rid of the train dirt. Then at three, when Proctor had gone on duty downstairs, she curled up, tucking her legs underneath, in one of the bedroom windows.

She was on the same side of the house as Proctor, with only a connecting bath between them; the south side. Under her was the riding ring. It was occupied now. A small figure wearing a white blouse, dark green jodhpurs and a red riding cap was trotting around and around, with equestrian gravity, on a black-and-white pony. A child who had everything, she remembered; and a child who'd had nothing. The familiar heaviness came back into her, perhaps a bit heavier than usual. She was still sitting there, and still looking down at little Elizabeth Burden, when Mrs. Bradley came in.

"Well, now," Mrs. Bradley began, glancing around first, and then making a minor but very critical adjustment on the blue-and-white tufted bedspread. "Here we are, and all settled, I hope. You've got everything that you want, dear?"

"Oh, yes," Ellen said, smiling back at her. She liked

40

Mrs. Bradley at once. Proctor had been correct in that, also. "Everything. Thank you."

"Then I'm glad," Mrs. Bradley said, patting her arm comfortably. "Very glad, dear. And they tell me that you helped to take care of Mrs. Cannaday in the hospital last month; so that part's going to be all right, isn't it? You're old friends."

"I hope we are," Ellen said. "And I don't mind the night duty at all. I think I prefer it."

"Then that's good, too," Mrs. Bradley said. "Because I don't believe that Miss Chisholm did. And the madam didn't seem to care very much for her, either; you could see that. But at times she does get a bit irritable, you know . . ." and she folded her hands over her waist, shaking her head at the thought, and looking vaguely troubled.

"I've seen days," she added, "when she doesn't want to have anyone at all speak to her. Not me, and I've been in the house with her for thirty-six years, mind you; not Mr. Burden; and not the child, even. Now that's not natural, of course; not in her. Would it be the medicine, do you think?"

"Perhaps so," Ellen agreed, for whatever comfort it brought. "Sometimes it does, Mrs. Bradley. They can't help it."

"I suppose they can't," Mrs. Bradley said, sighing deeply once more. "To be sure, dear." But she had wandered over to the window by this time, and there she brightened immediately. She pointed down at the riding ring, smiling broadly at Ellen over her right shoulder. "Now just look at that," she said, still pointing. "Ah, the sweet little love; her and her pony. But then she got it for her birthday, you know; and that was only . . . Let me see now. Was it . . . Yes. Of course. What's the matter with me? August 12th, that was. August 12th, dear. She was just seven years old."

41

And there was the second coincidence after that snapshot in Mrs. Cannaday's bedroom—the date of August 12, 1957. But a coincidence, only? After hearing it, in any event, Miss Ferguson smiled rather mechanically, walked out into the hall with Mrs. Bradley, and chatted for another minute or two. Then she came back in, closed the door after herself and sat down, also mechanically.

August 12, 1957 . . .

A lawnmower had begun chugging away on this side of the house; and very probably, within view of her bedroom window, a small figure was still jogging around down there on the black-and-white pony. Miss Ferguson did not look out at it, however; not again. A reasonable and intelligent caution seemed to be demanded of her.

August 12, 1957 . . .

She got up, with a confused idea that some act of physical urgency was required. What act? She could not imagine. She went into the bathroom, drank a glass of cold water and gave herself a slow, painful smile in the cabinet mirror. Yet why should it strike her as so extraordinary that a child had been born on that day to Mr. and Mrs. Robert Burden, just as another child, in very different circumstances, had been born either a few hours earlier or later over at 214 Maple Avenue? Perhaps five or six children had been born on that day, even in this small local area. Then why permit oneself to become so foolishly upset and excited about it? There was no connection, of course; not the slightest connection. Unless . . .

She returned to the bedroom, and discovered that she was still holding the empty glass. She put it down. Then she picked it up, tried to remember what it was and what she had been going to do with it—and put it down again. Unless what?

The question posed itself as if graven on stone before her; no avoiding it. All right, then. One dead child; one

living child. Simple as that, wasn't it? Unless, of course
—and suddenly her mind was able to move on from that
point as if it had begun working on its own now, with
no emotional relation to her—unless everyone at 214
Maple Avenue had lied to her seven years ago; even
Lucy. Even Lucy? But why would it have been necessary
for them to lie to her? It was true, of course, that Lucy
had never wanted her to keep the child, and that they
had argued and argued on that point—endlessly, bit-
terly. But still, and granting that part, Lucy could never
have . . .

She closed her eyes. No. Insane! But put it as a bare
supposition for the moment; nothing more. Could they
have lied to her, all three of them? Could they have got
together after the baby was born, and agreed on what
they should tell her about it? There was no question, at
any rate, but that a lie would have been ridiculously
simple under the circumstances that had prevailed over
there. She had held out against Lucy month after weary
month; but surely and certainly she could not be expected to hold out if they all told her that the baby had
died. Then what about the grave she had visited the
other morning?

She was in the bathroom again, still with that necessity for some physical movement in her. She groped for
the edge of the tub, found it and sat down on it. Just in
time, too; a wave of physical weakness had left her legs
quivering. The grave . . . But of course! What had she
been even thinking about? There was the grave, after
all—and the grave proved that a child had indeed died
on that August night seven years ago. But which child?
Or was considering that plain insanity again? Why
should one have been substituted for the other? Who
could have done such a thing? How could it have
been managed and arranged, for that matter? The bare
idea was fantastic. No!

But then, if the insanity of the idea had just been

admitted by Miss Ferguson, it was no longer a joke about that first-class psychiatrist. It was the plainest and most sickening truth, rather. She did need one; perhaps she had needed one for a long time. Because what had to be explained to her now, in a very soothing and gentle way, was that every so often, after childbirth, a mother would stubbornly refuse to admit that she had lost her baby. She would continue to believe, instead, and against all the hard factual evidence, that a mistake had been made, or else a deliberate substitution carried out. That was a well-known psychological phenomenon, one to be pitied and understood in other people. Whereas in oneself, it appeared now . . .

She got up, walked back into the bedroom and drew the shades. She lay down. But there was a complete lethargy in her, body and mind. She did not think about the picture any more, or about the date. Time passed. Now and again she shivered delicately, but with a very peculiar sense of being withdrawn from herself—from anything she should have felt at the moment, from even the simplest and most natural physical reaction. About five thirty Proctor came up, noticed the drawn shades, said "Oops," to herself, and tiptoed out quietly. More time passed. Then Proctor came up again at five minutes of seven. "Hey!" Proctor said, not quiet at all this time. "You trying to sleep around the clock, sweetie? Come on now. Upski, skibulski. You want to eat, don't you?"

So she went downstairs with Proctor, but with everything flickering in and out for her; unreal, shadowy. "What's the matter?" Proctor said. "You look a little funny to me. You feel all right, Fergy?" She smiled at Proctor, shaking her head, but not saying anything. "I know," Proctor said. "That crazy fresh air, eh? Just wait'll you eat something."

She tried to eat something. She followed Proctor into the room where they had been served lunch the

44

other day, and found Mrs. Bradley waiting for them, along with little Elizabeth Burden at last, and Miss Thornton, the English governess. She was introduced. She smiled at everyone. She sat down. And here and now, not imagined any more, but most solid flesh, Elizabeth Burden proved to be an active and high-spirited little girl, with a very independent manner for seven years old, a thin but healthily animated face and coolly reserved brown eyes. At once Proctor began to tease about the black-and-white pony, and she turned calmly and demurely from Miss Thornton, showed the tip of her tongue to Proctor with unmistakable impertinence, and then turned back calmly and demurely again as though nothing had happened. Proctor grinned. Apparently they got on very well together. After that Elizabeth glanced over at Miss Ferguson with appraising feminine curiosity, nothing else. There was no flash of puzzled but sure instinct between them; not on the child's part, very obviously; and not on hers, either, Ellen discovered. So she managed to steady a bit, unfolding her napkin—and became aware that Miss Thornton, a large, rather clumsy woman with a milky complexion and fair hair, had begun addressing her.

". . . although at home we do have a particular form of address for you people," Miss Thornton remarked. "Sister, you know," and she beamed over kindly. "Not Miss. I'm afraid it does seem just a little more befitting to me, for some reason. It clarifies a rather necessary social distinction, don't you see. And that's always rather a help for one, isn't it?"

"Oh, quait," Proctor drawled, eyeing her up and down grimly. "A help for two, even. And you people seem to have a potful of terms over there, don't you? I've heard tell you even call a nursemaid a nanny. Now in this neck of the woods, Elizabeth, a nanny is just an old goat, that's what—the kind that goes around all day butting at people. It doesn't know why, either. It just does it. It just keeps going baa-baa-baa all the time. Ever hear an old goat like that, did you?"

"Now, really," Miss Thornton said, beginning to spoon up her soup in a dainty and disapproving manner. "With the child."

"Then okay," Proctor said. "Just call it off, Gwendy. Who started this?"

Elizabeth stirred. She was across from Ellen, and eyeing her thoughtfully.

"I saw you before," she announced now. "In uniform, though. I saw you at the hospital last month. You were out at the desk; and you showed me how to read a fever thermomester."

"I did?" Ellen said. She felt a small, oddly cumbersome shock inside her. She looked up quickly; and then she also remembered. Relief swept into her like a whiff of pure oxygen, making her a bit dizzy for the moment. So here was the truth of the whole matter—the truth that she had indeed seen Miss Elizabeth Burden before. But to have it revealed to her by a seven-year-old child . . . She leaned forward hurriedly. The dizziness still bothered her a little.

"But I did," she repeated. "Of course! That's right. You were sitting on the hall bench, weren't you? And I said—"

"A thermomester," Miss Thornton put in. She shook her head over the word, sighing with exaggerated patience to herself. "Now, really," she said. "Really, child. We do happen to know just a little better than that, don't we?"

"A thermometer," Mrs. Bradley said. "A thermometer, dear."

"Well, anyway," Elizabeth said. "Whatever it was." She shrugged small shoulders, not disconcerted in any way; she seemed quite able to look out for herself, apparently, "I could be a nurse," she added, glancing coolly at Proctor this time, and then at Ellen. "When I grow up, of course. But I wouldn't hurt people by sticking those great ugly big needles into them. I just wouldn't, that's all. I think that's mean."

"Last week," Miss Thornton remarked, very gracious and condescending again, "you wanted to be an upstairs maid, if I remember correctly. A nurse, indeed! Miss Elizabeth Burden of Ridge Hill!"

"Okay," Proctor said. "Second round. Hey, Elizabeth. I bet you don't know what that old nanny goat does. And I just told you."

"I bet I do," Elizabeth said. "It goes baa-baa-baa all the time. There." She giggled a little, as if she and Proctor again understood one another quite perfectly. "Baa-baa-baa," she repeated, still giggling. "That's what it does. Baa-baa-baa. I think that's funny. Don't you, Miss Thornton?"

"I'm afraid not," Miss Thornton said, now icily severe with her. "I think it's something else. I think, miss, that it's vulgar and disgusting bad manners. A noise of that kind—and here at the dinner table. The very idea!"

She was extremely put out about it. She whisked Elizabeth upstairs immediately after dessert had been served, and Ellen followed them. The relief was still a bit shaky in her; she wanted to be alone for a time, without Proctor, even. So they had met at the hospital, after all—she and the child; and they had talked there for fifteen or twenty minutes. Then why wouldn't that snapshot have been bothersomely familiar to her? All the sick fancies had dissipated themselves suddenly. She smoked a cigarette, read for a while and then decided to close her eyes for just half an hour or so. But it was longer than that. She woke only at ten minutes before eleven, but woke sound and refreshed, the quiet and competent Miss Ferguson again. She dressed quickly—

47

cap, uniform, white stockings, rubber-soled white shoes
—and went down to Mrs. Cannaday's room.

Proctor was waiting for her.

"Now I told you about the medication this afternoon," Proctor whispered. "So that's okay. And you'll
find clean linen and everything in the bathroom closet,
if you have to change her. Do you want a cup of
coffee before you go in? I'll get it for you."

"Perhaps later," Ellen told her. "Thanks. Not now."

"Well," Proctor said, "they left it out on the kitchen
table for Chisholm, so help yourself. It's the instant
stuff. Give her another sleeping pill later on, if she gets
restless or uncomfortable. And of course check her temperature and her blood pressure right away if she acts
like she's getting a headache or a stiff neck; and then call
Dr. McCormick and tell him. I left his number over
there on the bedside table. That's about it, I guess. Just
keep your eyes open. See you tomorrow, sweetie."

She flitted off. She had left a lamp on in the bedroom,
the one on the writing desk, but she had tilted it away
from the other part of the room; this left the bed comfortably shaded for Mrs. Cannaday, who appeared to be
sleeping quietly when Ellen went in. Proctor had neatly
combed and brushed her gray hair, and changed her
into a fresh nightgown; she lay on her back, both arms
out over the coverlet, features in sharp upward profile.
Beside her was a small table with pills and medicine on
it—the spoon, the drinking glass, the carafe of ice water.
There was nothing for Ellen to do but refill the carafe at
the bathroom tap and then glance at the chart. After
that—it might have been just a bit cool in the room by
this time—she lowered two of the windows and sat down.

There was an evening paper on the desk, and a couple
of news magazines. She glanced at them. Presently the
big grandfather's clock out on the landing chimed
softly; half past eleven. But all the rest of the house was

48

now perfectly quiet, while in the sickroom itself there was nothing but the very familiar soft hush, yet with a certain urgent and watchful quality, that was always the same—an impression of something that was ticking away moment by moment; or else, in the soft, labored breathing that could be heard very faintly now, that was gathering in, perhaps. Twice Ellen moved over quietly to the bed, and looked down at Mrs. Cannaday. Neither time was there anything at all to do for her.

Twelve o'clock came. Then it was quiet outside, also. A car hummed distantly on the town road. Five minutes later another one followed it. Below was the dim glitter of the drive, lying in thick shadow. There was a black sky, with a few heavy stars shining; lonely dark woods all around; and then the river, with reflections of cold polished black on the surface, shifting and spreading out there in broad flashes, then shifting again, like silent and obscure night signals. Way over on the opposite shore a few lights could be seen, remote pinpricks in all of the infinite surrounding darkness.

About one o'clock the patient roused briefly, with the petulant whine that indicated fretful and bewildered half-consciousness. But she wanted nothing when Ellen went over to her. She only sent up a dull, fuddled glance, whimpered again and closed her eyes. Later still, about one thirty, a car came up the Ridge Hill driveway, and was driven around to the big garage in back. A few minutes after that, someone rapped at the hall door. It was Robert Burden. He hesitated a moment, obviously having expected Tottie Chisholm, then came in.

There was a faint, spicy odor of cigarettes and Scotch whiskey about him. She could see no physical evidence that he had been drinking, however. He wore a white dinner jacket and a black tie, and moved with the heavy-shouldered, almost slouchy physical ease that she had remembered in him. And there was still that distasteful impression of carefully tended bodily sleekness—the smooth sandy hair, the square, deeply tanned face, the hard flesh under the eyes, the crisp, ruddy mustache. He nodded at her.

"So we don't have Miss Chisholm any more," he said. A slow, deep voice, stolid and inexpressive; a dull but perhaps sharply appraising glance from the brown eyes; a nod of the head.

"No, we don't," Ellen said. "She left today, Mr. Burden."

He nodded again, still appraising her.

"Well, that's all right," he said, keeping his voice low for Mrs. Cannaday's benefit, and deciding to smile finally, but a slow, vague smile that was not really interested in proving itself. "We'll try not to miss her too much, won't we? And I don't imagine we will, somehow. You're Miss Ferguson, of course. You've got everything you need up here?"

So Proctor had not been mistaken about that, either. He remembered Miss Ferguson; that nice, quiet Miss Ferguson. But it did not appear that he remembered her in the way that she remembered him; because now, even more strongly than at the hospital a month ago, she was aware of a deep-rooted and quite instinctive personal dislike of the man. She would, in any event, have disliked what he had just said. It was not altogether a reflection on Tottie Chisholm, since he had been careful enough to leave that opening for himself; but it was certainly, on the shortest possible acquaintanceship, a rather unmistakable compliment for Tottie Chisholm's successor. She had been standing over by the hall door since he entered. She remained there. But perhaps, to make such a casually offhanded attempt to impress her with the Robert Burden affability just now, his true opinion of her might be that nice, stupid Miss Ferguson. Was that what he had really wanted up here?

50

"Yes," she said. "Yes, I have. Thank you." Then she glanced at her watch, letting him see that she did. It was twenty minutes of two. He might have understood the implied professional rebuke in that action; he might not. He showed no sign of what it meant to him, either way.

"I'm afraid it's rather late," she said, making it altogether plain to him this time. "And I don't think she ought to be disturbed, Mr. Burden. She needs her rest."

"Then we won't disturb her, of course," he agreed. "She's had a pretty good night so far?"

"I believe so," Ellen told him. "Since eleven o'clock, anyway. Yes, she has."

She was still over by the hall door; still, very apparently, waiting to close it after him. He considered that, head down, smiling vaguely. Then he roused.

"Fine," he said. "Fine. I liked to check with Miss Chisholm when I came in. She always expected me." He moved out into the hall finally, and paused there. "She rather worried Miss Chisholm," he added evenly. "She got restless, and wanted things; and she's a little difficult to understand, of course. That's the sad part, unfortunately. Well . . ."

There was great deftness in it. The direct question was not put as to whether she had wanted anything from Miss Ferguson tonight; and yet waiting another moment, but just long enough so that the waiting would not become obvious to Miss Ferguson, the implication was there. It was not responded to, however. Miss Ferguson said nothing at all.

Again he roused himself.

"Well, that's the way it is," he said, having decided, perhaps, that Miss Ferguson was not the sparkling and alert type, mentally. "I'll see her tomorrow morning, then. Good night. Good night, Miss Ferguson."

"Good night," she said. "Good night, Mr. Burden."

51

She closed the door after him. They had both spoken in low, carefully guarded tones; and yet it appeared that they had managed to disturb Mrs. Cannaday, after all. She was still lying on her back, but her head had turned a little toward Ellen now, and her good hand was jerking up, with much shaky effort, as if to point out something or other on the bedside table. Ellen moved over quickly.

"Is there anything you want me to do?" she asked. "Perhaps some water, Mrs. Cannaday?"

It had been a very small physical effort; yet Mrs. Cannaday had to rest for a moment. Then the hand jerked once again, and she glared up at Ellen with the deceptively savage expression of the sick and befuddled. Her lips quivered. Nothing came out. She lost patience with herself. She began to breathe hurriedly, with an effect of febrile excitement.

Water, Ellen decided. She poured some from the carafe, put a fresh drinking tube into the glass and raised Mrs. Cannaday's head gently. But it was not water that Mrs. Cannaday wanted. She collected herself, breath whistling, and made another attempt.

She pointed behind Ellen.

Over on that side of the room there could be seen a chair, a love seat, the fireplace and the fireplace mantel. On the mantelpiece were two white China candlesticks, a small clock, a picture or two—and the framed snapshot of little Elizabeth Burden.

The snapshot, then? Proctor had said never to remove it from the bedside table, but Proctor must have forgotten her own warning. Now, however, as soon as the snapshot had been brought back, Mrs. Cannaday stared fixedly at it. Then she reached out, touching it. It was a rather odd gesture—fumbling, tender, and yet feverishly excited still. She tried to say something, but produced nothing more than a hoarse, choking sound. She began to cry. Then she made another attempt, drawing back into herself with a kind of desperate exasperation—and so breaking through finally and triumphantly.

"No," she whispered, if Ellen understood her at all. "Not . . . Monica's. Not . . . the . . . child. No. Must . . . must . . ."

But after that, as soon as she had pronounced the words, they appeared to lose all importance for her. She sighed, pushing fretfully at Ellen to get away now; and yet what she had just said appeared to ring off against the stillness in the room on softer and softer echoes—a low, broken, infinitely mournful protest. She closed her eyes, the heavy tears still glistening on her cheeks. She whimpered one last time, holding Ellen. Then, outside, very softly and carefully—in the direction of Robert Burden's room, was it?—a door closed.

FIVE

WELL, NO," said Miss Cotter. "No." It was early the next morning; she had just driven out from town for the seven-to-three duty with Mrs. Cannaday; and she and Ellen were chatting for a minute or two up in the second-floor corridor—if that could be considered as exactly the befitting term with Miss Cotter. But they had begun by talking about the small hospital in town, and they had now reached the point where Miss Ferguson had inquired, though with only a very mild outward interest, as to whether or not Elizabeth Burden had been born there.

"No, she wasn't," Miss Cotter repeated, her starched

54

cap somewhat askew, and her gray little peanut head a little over to one side in a bright, perkily assured attitude. "You see, Mrs. Burden was supposed to go down to a big specialist in New York when her time came; but then there wasn't any chance to do it like that, everything happened so fast. So the child was born right in this house as a matter of fact, and Mrs. Burden died here the next morning. They wanted me in attendance, you know; only I couldn't. Oh, yes. Poor, delicate little thing. Everyone liked her. But of course she should never have had the child at all, if you want my opinion of it. That's what did it, you know. That's what finished her."

And she rambled on about what Dr. McCormick had said and done; about the funeral, and the people present for it; about all the flowers. Ellen listened to that, too, not to alert Miss Cotter in her direction now, since apparently it was no trick at all to alert Miss Cotter in any other; but by then the one vitally important fact had been established for her. A hospital would have been required to keep certain records: the blood type of the Burden child, its physical condition at birth, its footprints. Such marks of identification would not have been necessary at Ridge Hill, however. Only one child had been born here, and that one to Mr. and Mrs. Robert Burden. So . . .

She went upstairs to her room, all the dark, ugly uncertainties back again and darker than ever. Proctor got up at about a quarter of eight, padded around in the connecting bathroom between their rooms and then stuck her head in.

"Sweetie?" she called out. "Hey! You aren't asleep yet, are you? What kind of a night did you have?"

But Ellen was turned from her on the bed, and remained turned. She did not answer. She was still awake, though, when Proctor went down to breakfast; and awake when Proctor came back, for that matter. Lucy; the house over on Maple Avenue; Katie Stoner . . . Had any records been kept over there, either? Perhaps a few necessary ones. A child had been buried from that address, after all; and so there would have to be at least a birth certificate and a death certificate. Then Katie Stoner would have to be asked about them, to settle the matter once and for all. But to confront that woman again, and in that house . . .

At nine o'clock she got up and took a sleeping pill. At ten o'clock she took another one. But that was a rather serious mistake on her part. She slept afterward, but with heavy and disturbed restlessness. She woke often from badly confused dreams of one kind or another, and got up at half past three in the afternoon with nothing but a dull, thick-headed tiredness in her.

She took a long shower for that; very hot first, and afterward ice cold. It helped somewhat. Then she went downstairs, using the elevator to avoid any chance at all of encountering Proctor in the second-floor corridor. No Dr. Bennett was listed now in the local phone book, she found out; but there was still a Mrs. Joseph A. Stoner at 214 Maple Avenue.

She closed the book. So; there it was. Very easy to settle now, the whole thing; or, on the other hand, to turn deliberately away from, if she wanted no trouble about it. Which? Trying to decide, she found herself listening to the small activities of the house around her; Mrs. Bradley's voice, steps out in the kitchen passage, a door closing. It made her think of another door closing only a few hours ago, but very quietly and carefully; of dull little brown eyes studying her. That decided the matter. She opened the book again, dialed the local cab company and then waited out on the gravel turnaround.

Yet there was a little reasonable caution in her. She did not have the cab take her to Maple Avenue, but left it at the town shopping center, and then walked. Cowardice again? A shrinking desire to put off this meeting with Katie Stoner until the last possible moment? She pushed ahead quickly, not to examine her own motives too much, perhaps not to be tempted again; and at ten minutes of four opened a gate, walked up a flagstoned path and rang the front doorbell at 214 Maple Avenue.

There was movement back in the hall. Then Katie Stoner could be seen, waddling forward placidly.

"Yes?" she said.

The house at 214 might have changed considerably in physical detail. Katie Stoner had not. The voice was still small and sweet, pipingly childlike in tone; and the face, too, plump and round, with the thickly lustrous black hair coiled over it, and the fine, creamy complexion, had something of a little girl's softness and prettiness. She peered out at Ellen through the screen door. "Yes?" she repeated. She wore a fresh and unwrinkled blue dress with a gold watch pinned on front and a dab of French lace at the throat. She was fondling the watch with a rather stagy *grande dame* effect. It was quite obvious that she had not recognized Ellen. So it was a little difficult to start off on the right note.

"I wonder," Ellen heard herself begin awkwardly, "I wonder if . . . You don't remember me, of course. But I . . . Well, I'd like to talk to you inside, Mrs. Stoner. Could I? It's rather private."

The little girl's face remained tranquil. The black eyes, still smiling out with a placidly deceptive sweetness, might have sharpened a bit.

"Rather private," Katie Stoner said. "Oh, my." She stood motionless in the hall, debating with herself. "Then all right," she said, at last opening the screen door, and at the same moment glancing up and down Maple Avenue casually. "Come in. But watch the step there. You're not selling anything?"

"No," Ellen said. "No, I'm not."

They went into the living room on the right. Seven years ago, outside and in, the Stoner nursing home had been all furtive and untidy dinginess; a few pieces of cheap rattan furniture, faded brown oilcloth in the hall, a spotted and worn grass rug in the living room. Now everything was much different. Raspberry-red wall-to-wall carpeting, for one detail; a big new television set for another; an oversized aquarium in the window, with brilliantly colored tropical fish swimming around in it; a couch and two easy chairs with striped slip covers on them; and a glass clock on the mantel, the insides all visible and chugging away, which was elegantly set off by a few shiny black figurines on each side. Katie Stoner sat down on the couch, opened a box of chocolates that was lying before it on a marble-topped coffee table, and chose a big butter cream. She was quite placid about that, also. The candy box was not offered to Ellen. It was set down on her lap comfortably, and kept there.

"But you're not from town," she remarked, biting into the cream and then licking the tip of her finger in a dainty, refined manner. "Or are you? I think you do seem a little familiar to me. Only I can't quite—"

"It's been rather a long time," Ellen told her. She had begun smiling effortfully, without wanting to smile, without wanting to concede even that much to the Stoner woman; yet altogether unable to help herself. "But I'm . . ." And then there was a stricken instant during which she could not remember whatever name it was that Lucy had given here seven years ago. She had to grope for it, the black eyes twinkling roguishly at her. "But I'm Mrs. Franklin," she said. "And I—well, I had a child here some years ago. It's about that."

"There," Katie Stoner said, still tranquil. "I knew I remembered you. A little boy, wasn't it?"

"A little girl," Ellen corrected her. "My sister Lucy

58

was with me. She made the arrangements. You'd remember her, probably."

"Oh?" Katie Stoner said. The doll's face became even more smilingly vacuous; a mask of rosy, grotesquely plump dough over the blue dress and the red-and-white candy box. She picked out another cream, inspected it and put it back. That gave her time to reflect suitably, perhaps. At last she stirred, holding the candy box in both hands. She put it down on the coffee table. She replaced the cover.

"Oh, yes," she said. "Now I do remember. But I'm sorry, Mrs. . . . Mrs. Franklin, was it?" And her eyes lifted from the candy box, sly and demure again, after having hesitated for exactly the same fraction of time that Ellen had hesitated. "Very sorry. Because you see I don't run the nursing home any more. I haven't in years. So if it's anything like that again . . ."

She shook her head primly. But of course it was not necessary to finish the sentence. Her tone had already indicated to Ellen, with this new primness of hers, what that was.

"No," Ellen said. She had flushed a bit, being very silly again; but almost at once a certain disgusted contempt for the other woman made itself felt, and steadied her beautifully. "No, it isn't," she said. "It's something else."

"Something else," Mrs. Stoner repeated. "Is that right?" She fingered the gold watch, shoulders back, face placid, as if again trying for the serene dowager effect; but now, of course, there had been a declaration made and accepted between them. They each knew it. Katie Stoner, therefore, shifted herself the least bit, in obvious preparation for whatever would develop from now on.

"I see," she went on. "Not that again. Well, I'm glad, you know, very glad, because there happened to be an-

59

other girl in here talking to me only last week. Oh, a pretty little thing. So sweet! And I did feel sorry for her. Still, I wasn't much help, I'm afraid. I couldn't even recommend anyone."

She leaned forward, a bit roguish now, and resumed in a lower and more confidential manner; intimate woman-to-woman talk.

"I wasn't permitted," she explained, shaking her head firmly. "Oh, dear, no. Because you see there's a friend that I have, a gentleman friend; and you just wouldn't believe how annoyed he got about the whole business. He's very particular, you know; very touchy about the company I permit myself these days. But he happened to drop by while we were talking here in this room, and just about this time of the day, too. Yes. Almost four thirty, isn't it? That's his usual. Oh, he was dreadful! A common little gutter tart, he called that poor girl. You couldn't even imagine what he said. Everybody in the whole block must have heard him. But that's it, you see. That's his way. He comes straight to the point."

A warning, Ellen realized. Persist now, and the gentleman friend who was expected at four thirty would come straight to the point with her, also—and so emphatically that everyone in the whole block would hear him. Did she understand that?

She did. She persisted, however. The anger and the contempt were still solidly helpful.

"But I'm trying to tell you," she began again. "It isn't that at all, Mrs. Stoner. My sister wanted to put out the child for adoption that time, and I wouldn't agree. So after it was born—"

"Oh, a family matter," Katie Stoner interrupted. "I see. Yes. Well, I can't help you at all about that, I'm afraid. I just don't seem to remember, somehow; not a thing. I am sorry."

"Perhaps if you tried," Ellen suggested, again smil-

ing effortfully, and again despising herself. "If I reminded you, Mrs. Stoner. Just a question or two, that's
all. Very simple questions. Because I was told—"

"Simple or not, no." Katie Stoner interrupted once
more, even more calmly. "And I just told you—so that's
all. Now, please."

She got up, waddled over to the screen door in the
hall and opened it, thus indicating that the matter was
finished between them.

"It's not my business," she added. "Not my business
at all. But I do think that if I found myself so terribly
interested in it all of a sudden, Mrs.—well, whatever you
called yourself—I'd talk to my sister about it. I would,
really. Not to me."

The plump little face had turned stone hard. The
smile had vanished. The warning, this time, was plain,
ominous and direct.

"But if I've done that already?" Ellen asked her. She
had risen also, to face Katie Stoner, and to make the lie
fully convincing between them. "And I'm very much
afraid that I have," she went on grimly. "That was the
first step, you understand—to make her admit what you
did. You told me that the child had died, all of you,
because my sister knew that I'd never agree to the other
thing. Now I believe that makes it a police matter; and I
think I'd bear that in mind, Mrs. Stoner. But you still
can't remember anything?"

A pause. A very brief pause, too; just two or three
dead seconds between them in the front hall at 214
Maple Avenue—and yet, at the end of it, a heavy and
trapped pause. After it, quite suddenly, Mrs. Stoner
waddled back toward Ellen, rosebud mouth twisted up,
pudgy little fists clenched.

"Now who sent you to me?" she demanded breathlessly. "Did he? Did that drunken old sot of a Willie
Bennett? Is that it? You and your sister! But come off

that, if you know who you're talking to. Dirty, cunning little blackmailing sluts, the two of you. Down on your knees whining and begging to me that time, to take you in; and now, just because of a drunken old fool who doesn't know what he's talking about, to get the idea into your heads that there might be a spot of money around somewhere. Oh, don't I know you! Just find out who the parents are now, who I gave it to—because that's the idea, isn't it? And then put the squeeze against them. Well, think again. I know the story you have ready for me, every one of you! That you're married now, all right and proper; that you want your own dear little toddler again, to love and to cherish; and that if I don't admit to you who the parents are— Well, I won't. I won't, I tell you. So go on now. You get out of this house!"

She had worked herself into passionate physical excitement by this time. She came forward another step, got hold of Ellen by the right arm and the left shoulder and spun her viciously out past the screen door. The porch railing was out there, fortunately. Ellen found herself crouching against it, unable to move for the moment.

"But I wanted my child," she whispered back, anything else, in the complete mental and physical paralysis she felt now, not even remotely within reach. "And you lied to me, all of you. I wanted my child!"

"Then you know where to look," Katie Stoner breathed out venomously, slamming the screen door between them. "Where you buried it. It's still there. Oh, no fear! So go over to the Town Hall now, and check the birth certificate; and then, while you're at it, check the death certificate. And tell Willie Bennett something from me, if he's putting you up to this thing—that it's *his* name on file for what happened, and not mine. I know what you're trying here, the lot of you. I know the game, I tell you. But if you think Katie Stoner's the kind to play it with you . . ."

She glared out, eyes glittering.

"And don't you ever come back to this house," she breathed. "So mind that now, you and your sister— because if you don't, there might be someone I know who'd crack your neck for you with his two hands. Yes. By God he would! And that's the one warning you'll get. *You keep away!*"

The inside door was slammed. The inside shade on it was pulled down. Then Ellen managed to turn, to go out through the gate, to cross the road and to glance back numbly from perhaps a third of a block distant. At once curtains were pulled into place at the living-room window, but not before she had seen Katie Stoner still watching her from back there, and still scared and furious. The right fist lifted again; threatened savagely again; then nothing.

She turned, not quite groping a way for herself, although with a confused idea that it might be necessary to do that at any moment. There was a small park on the corner of Main Street. She went into it, sat down on the first bench and discovered that she was shaking now, not very much, perhaps, but all over; a fine and persistent inner nervous vibration. Yet it did not affect her in any way. She appeared to be sitting a little apart, as it were; not quite in contact. What mattered to her was a simple declarative sentence of just four words. The child was alive. The child was alive. The child was alive.

Presently she managed to acquire a little sensible detachment. The Town Hall, she remembered. She got up, walked back down Main Street to the one traffic light in town and asked a policeman. The Town Hall was just around the corner. But in there she discovered immediately that Katie Stoner was on very firm ground, indeed; everything correct and in good order, as she had promised it would be. There was a birth certificate for an infant Franklin under the date of August 12, 1957; and there was a death certificate for the same child on the day following. Both documents had been filled out and signed by a William J. Bennett, M.D.

"Doc Bennett?" the clerk said. She was a dry, brisk woman, the perfect example of officious insolence, and now she permitted herself to show the insolence. "Well," she drawled deliberately. "I don't know just where you would find him. He's left town, you know; lost his license to practice a couple of years ago. Something about young girls, they tell me. Police thing. But you wanted Doc Bennett in particular, did you?"

"In particular," Ellen said. "That's right. Thank you."

It was quite clear what the clerk thought of her for that preference. She did not care, however. It seemed now, indeed, that she could have faced any shame or humiliation, after Katie Stoner, without flinching from them; even that she deserved such things. Because why had she made a few simple inquiries about the child only this afternoon, and not seven years ago, when the thing had happened? But perhaps she had held off for a very obvious reason. Perhaps she had suspected about the child all along. Was that it? She might have believed Lucy and Dr. Bennett then because it had been the easy way out for her. But inevitably, if that were so, she had abandoned the child in a colder and more callous manner than Lucy had abandoned it. Then she also had acted a part, and perfectly: quiet, heartbreaking sorrow; simple and courageous dignity. While year after year, in the heart, very deep in, and never once admitted to herself, even for a moment . . .

She paused on the front steps, feeling a bit physically nauseated at the idea, as if she had become aware now, without warning, of an infinite vileness in herself. Yet what did she want to understand, really? The truth, that was all. Only what was the truth? Had she believed what they told her seven years ago, or hadn't she?

It was impossible for her to say. What she faced now, layer beneath layer, was an ugly complexity of human motive, nothing clear and decided at all, nothing that she could accept for herself as proven fact. So another realization was forced on her, and a more appalling one. Then it was possible. Then she could have suspected the thing all along. And yet . . . and yet there had been excuses enough, if excuses were necessary to her. When was a woman half so vulnerable and defenseless as in childbirth, or immediately afterward? When was there such utter dependence on other people to look out for her, and to look out for the child? So she had that small, bitter comfort, at any rate.

And then she had trusted Lucy, if no one else. She had! And she had insisted on visiting the grave that time. So for that part there might have been a very feeble excuse. But for the other, now that she knew the truth, finally, or a portion of it? How could there be comfort for her ever again after today if she abandoned the child for the second time in her life, and with full knowledge that it was alive at this moment, either happy or unhappy, either wanted or miserable? Only . . . where was it by this time? *Who* was it? Because of course that was what she would have to determine first of all, and through Katie Stoner. There was the one possible starting point.

A corner lunchroom stood opposite the Town Hall. She walked over to it, ordered tea and toast at the counter and made another attempt to consider sensibly. Katie Stoner, she was able to decide then, had defied her this afternoon from the most obvious necessity. But how could Katie Stoner defy Lucy, who must have known all about the arrangements that had been made—who, indeed, must have been a prime party to them? No. Katie Stoner's position was not quite so impregnable as it appeared, despite the death certificate. Very probably, over the years, and in a small rural community of this size, there must have been more than a few whispers about 214 Maple Avenue. The local police, then, must know a little something about it, and about Katie Stoner. Yet, even if they did, it would be necessary to furnish them with solid material proof before they could take any official action in the matter.

And where was the proof? Nowhere at all, because Katie Stoner appeared to know well enough how to protect herself in such matters. She had specialized in lonely and desperate young girls, cut off from all ordinary counsel of friend or family; and so it would not have been at all difficult for her to persuade or cajole them into doing whatever she wanted them to do. Although with Lucy, of course, who had already been urging the same thing, very little cajolement would have been necessary.

"Now I know how it is," Katie Stoner might have suggested to her, with that hypocritical sweetness and sympathy. "And I do feel so sorry for you; for both of you. But tell me: Did you ever think of having the child turned over to someone? Did you? Now I'm not urging it, of course. Do whatever you think right. But it's been done many a time before, remember—and in the long run it's best for everybody concerned, as I see it. You'd have no medical expenses for one thing, not a penny; and there might even be a few dollars handed over so that the poor little thing in there would have some kind of a chance to put herself back on her feet again. And I could promise you that the child would get a fine, decent home. Oh, yes. Perfectly respectable people. They're always after me. Why, you wouldn't believe who some of them are. But you think about it, that's all.

66

And then, of course, we'll make it whatever you want, dear. Do you see?"

Because certainly one had read of such things—of establishments like 214 Maple Avenue, and of women like Katie Stoner, who ran a thriving, under-the-counter business in black-market babies. There were people who wanted children, and every once in a while they were people who could not adopt them through legitimate channels because one or both of the parents were divorced, or ill, or a little too old. So in the end, having been rejected by the authorized agencies, those people resorted to someone like Katie Stoner; and at 214 Maple Avenue there would be very few questions asked—not even their right names, perhaps. There would be only a cash payment, nothing else; whatever could be extracted from them.

But concede now that the child had been disposed of in such a manner; sold, actually. Then there might be an even more hopeless problem: Katie Stoner might have no idea in the world where to look for the child. And that could be why, after trying to evade all questions this afternoon, she had bullied and threatened. Not because she had wanted to protect the child in its new life, or protect the parents; but simply and horribly —oh, dear Lord!—because after seven years its whereabouts were completely unknown to her. Unless, of course, it had been accepted somehow or other as little Elizabeth Burden of Ridge Hill. And then it wouldn't have been only a matter of four or five hundred dollars paid over to Katie Stoner as a quitclaim, not with the Cannaday millions involved in the thing. It would have been a lot more than that. There was Katie Stoner's new car, after all, and the comfortably genteel prosperity these days at 214 Maple Avenue. Someone must have paid for those things, and paid well. Who was it?

She went back outside, leaving her tea and toast. It

was beginning to cloud up now, with distant thunder rumbling and growling, but she was scarcely conscious of that. And what about the child itself? she had begun thinking. Because now, most important of all, it was the child who would matter here. Seven years old by this time, whoever and wherever she was, there might be parents to whom she felt affectionately devoted. It might even prove out that she was indeed little Elizabeth Burden of Ridge Hill, with everything in the world waiting for her. Then what should be done? What sudden motherly closeness could be offered to a child of that age, without any preparation at all—and offered seven years after the child had really needed that closeness?

She began to realize some of the endless complexities that were rising up before her. And what should she do about them? Call Lucy? Find out what Lucy had known? Nothing else came to her at the moment. She walked ahead to the shopping center and the village drugstore, closeted herself in one of the two booths at the back and called New York.

But there was no answer from the shop at this hour, well after five, nor from the apartment. She waited a few minutes and tried the apartment again, just as futilely. That time, when she came out of the phone booth, she saw Robert Burden and little Elizabeth standing over by the prescription counter.

There was a side entrance back of the perfume display. She used it. But it was beginning to rain now, a sudden afternoon shower, and that trapped her. The door opened again, as she hesitated a moment on the covered walk outside. They appeared behind her.

Today he was wearing a light summer suit, a dotted bow tie and a Panama hat. It seemed to Miss Ferguson that he had not recognized her out of the nurse's uniform; but he had. He was only making up his mind whether or not to acknowledge the recognition. He said: "Good afternoon," finally, giving her the same vague, not really interested smile as last night, and then touching his hat. "Coming down, I'm afraid. We couldn't offer you a lift, Miss Ferguson?"

"No, thank you," Miss Ferguson said. She managed somehow or other to smile back, and to offer the first plausible excuse that presented itself. "Miss Proctor asked me to do a little shopping for her. I was looking for the dime store."

"Oh?" he said. He was holding a long, thin cigar perfectly level in two fingers of his right hand. Now he pointed with it. "Over there," he said. "But they seem to be closing, I'm afraid. It's five thirty."

And it was. The window lights had been turned off, and a man was locking the front door behind him.

"Do it tomorrow," Robert Burden suggested to her. "This might keep up for a while. I'll get the car. You wait right here with Miss Ferguson, Libby."

"Hi," Elizabeth said. It was obviously a contradiction in terms to think of a seven-year-old child as being indifferently remote and unapproachable, if she wanted to be; and yet the impression had been made on Miss Ferguson during dinner last night, and was made again now. There was a colored poster in the drugstore window behind them, and the child was studying it with grave adult composure. "That's for the fair," she explained, also gravely. "It's going to be in Rhinebeck next week. Do you like fairs?"

"Well, yes, I do," Miss Ferguson said. Her one desire had been to be left quite alone for a time—somewhere, anywhere; even now she did not feel in full and effective control of herself. She steadied a bit. "Very much," she added. "Are you going with your father?"

"Oh, no, he wouldn't," Elizabeth said, putting the statement as a very plain matter of fact, without emphasis. Then she glanced around at the car, also indifferently —at the face turned to them now from the front seat, but not within hearing distance, the Panama hat shading it, the cigar in the mouth. "I wouldn't even ask him," she said. "But you know what they have? They have a big swing, and they let two people stand up in it and push as hard as they can. I saw two men that went all the way around in it last year. They gave them a prize."

The car came. She jumped in back, allowing Miss Ferguson to sit up front with Robert Burden. Then she leaned forward a little, swinging herself on both elbows.

"I went with Miss Thornton," she confided. "Only she didn't want to go very much. She has to put arches in her shoes. Sometimes her feet just kill her, she told Mrs. Bradley."

"I've told you about that before," Robert Burden said, taking the cigar out of his mouth. "Don't make everything that you hear an intimate topic of conversation with other people. That's enough now. Sit back there."

He sounded a bit sharp and annoyed about it, and then appeared to become conscious that he had not hit on exactly the right note with Miss Ferguson present. He glanced at her, and lightened his tone playfully; but that was not altogether on key, either. One corrected a small child, Miss Ferguson was telling herself; but not, unless it were a habit of long standing, with such automatic and palpable distaste for having to correct it.

"Please," he said. "Why can't you remember, Libby? Miss Thornton has to keep her own little secrets, you know. Where did she take you?"

They swung out into Main Street. Elizabeth, chin on hands, looked up at him in rather a puzzled fashion.

"We were talking about the fair," she explained carefully. "That's all."

"Oh, the fair," Robert Burden said. The crisp British

70

mustache smiled now in just the proper way at Miss
Ferguson; and yet the idea given, whether justified or
not, was that he wanted to include himself in the conversation very smoothly and deftly. The stern father a
moment ago, when necessity bade; the indulgent one
now. Quite understood, wasn't it? "Yes," he said.
"They're having it next week, aren't they? So you plan
to go down with Miss Thornton, do you?"

"Oh, I don't know," Elizabeth said. She kept her chin
on her hands, but stared straight ahead at the road now,
her expression indifferent once more. "I went last year
with her. I don't care."

"Now, now," Robert Burden said, again glancing
amusedly at Miss Ferguson; a private and indulgent
communication between adults. "You don't care a bit,
do you? Not at all, Libby?"

Miss Ferguson smiled back at him. It was the thing to
do, obviously. But what struck her was the complete
change-over in Elizabeth. One moment, when alone
with Miss Ferguson, she had wanted very much to go to
the fair; then next moment, with Robert Burden, she
was apparently trying to pass it off as a matter of disin-
terest to her.

"But I take it that we don't want to go this time with
Miss Thornton," he went on amiably. "I see. But why,
Libby?"

And then Miss Ferguson began to get another impression from all this, a not quite credible impression. It
seemed to her that there was something of a contest here
between father and daughter; that an easy adult attack
had been made, and that a wary and almost sullen defense was being set up against it.

"Because," Elizabeth said, taking refuge at last in the
one perfect child's reason. "That's why. I'd like to go
with Miss Proctor. She's loads of fun. She'd never get
tired."

"Oh," Robert Burden said, drawling a bit. "Yes.

71

Loads of fun. I see the point, but I don't know that I'd quite express it in that way. However . . ."

He smiled ahead at the road this time.

"What?" Elizabeth said. Then she shrugged small shoulders, dismissing him for the moment, and turned to Miss Ferguson. "But I do like her," she said earnestly. "We go for a walk sometimes. Is she a good friend of yours?"

"Yes, she is," Miss Ferguson said. "We used to room together."

"Well, then," Elizabeth said. She considered a moment. "I have a friend, too," she added. "Barbara Ann. But do you know what we do? We fight sometimes. She's like a baby, though. She cries afterward. Would you cry if somebody did something to you?"

"I hope not," Miss Ferguson said, her smile becoming painfully fixed for some reason. "I'd try not to."

"I don't," Miss Elizabeth Burden said, chin up, not even looking at him this time. "And they couldn't make me. I'd say ha-ha, that's all. I just wouldn't care."

There was another almost imperceptible jar among the three of them; something not right in this conversation, something a bit twisted. Robert Burden realized it, too. He shifted himself.

"Now that's the spirit," he said, still amiable and indulgent, still working for the impression he wanted in Miss Ferguson. "Good girl. But if I wanted to go to the fair with Miss Proctor, I'd ask her myself. Why don't you?"

"What?" Elizabeth asked. She turned quickly, facing him. Then it might have been the wariness again, or the never quite comprehensible operation of a small mind. She caught herself.

"Oh, maybe I will," she said. "I don't know. I could, couldn't I?"

"I don't know why not," Robert Burden said. "But how about Miss Ferguson? How about me? Perhaps Mrs.

72

Bradley could pack a luncheon basket for us. Chicken sandwiches. We could make it a picnic."

"Oh, yes," Elizabeth cried, all defenses forgotten. "Would you? Would you, Miss Ferguson? Just the three of us. Just you and me and Miss Proctor. Because he wouldn't, you know; he only says that. Oh, please, Miss Ferguson!"

But she had used the "he" again, before an outsider this time, and both he and Miss Ferguson understood the telltale effect of that impersonal pronoun from Elizabeth. The big hands tightened a bit on the steering wheel. He was annoyed. He was very much annoyed. The almost paralyzing thing was that he decided to hit back. And why not? There was only that nice, stupid Miss Ferguson riding along in the car with them.

"Well, I suppose he wouldn't," Robert Burden said, speaking a little more softly than before, with the carefully veiled adult softness of contempt and dislike. "He's only saying that. I see. But then perhaps he might find something to say about if and when Miss Thornton can spare the time to take you to the fair next week. I think I've warned you about your impertinence before. It's getting beyond bounds, I'm afraid. Now sit down back there and start behaving yourself."

And of course it was childish impertinence. But it was something else, too. It had given back blow for blow, contempt for contempt and dislike for dislike. Miss Elizabeth Burden might not have known what to make of the heavy playfulness in him; but she knew what to make of this attitude. Here at last was the established relationship between them. She proved it out by her reaction to it.

"Oh, I'd rather," she said, swinging herself forward again, but just once, to show him, clearly. "I don't care; and I don't care about that old fair, either. I wouldn't even go with Miss Thornton. Ha-ha."

She sat down in the back seat, and hummed airily to

herself all the way up the Ridge Hill driveway. There they pulled around to the side entrance, and Miss Ferguson got out.

"Thank you," she said. She spoke carefully, knowing that she had to be very careful now, not to show anything; and she was. But she knew better than to look at a small figure slouched down in the back seat, still humming to itself, or even to speak to it. Only a few hours ago, Miss Ferguson had been called on to risk almost her full limit with Katie Stoner; and so it did not seem even faintly advisable to risk it again here and now with Mr. Robert Burden. Father and daughter drove around to the garage in back. She entered the house. And of course Proctor and Mrs. Bradley had to be down in the front hall, discussing something or other. They both heard her come in. They both turned.

"So you're finally back, are you?" Proctor demanded. She must have been a bit miffed about Miss Ferguson's disappearance that afternoon. She put both hands on her hips. "A fine thing," she declared indignantly. "Just where did you sneak off to today without a word to anyone? What did you do?"

It was difficult to face even Proctor at this moment; then how much more difficult, it came to Miss Ferguson, to face dinner tonight, and the child again. She backed off a little, shaking her head quickly, and smiling at them.

"In town," she said. "I had something to mail, Proctor. That's all."

"That's what all?" Proctor persisted, following after her. "You wait a minute. What's the matter with you? What's wrong, Fergy?"

"Nothing," Miss Ferguson said. Over by the elevator now, she felt safer and more secure with distance between them. "Nothing," she repeated. She got the door open.

74

"Now I hope you didn't go and get yourself caught in the rain," Mrs. Bradley put in, looking immediately concerned at the possibility. "Is that it? You look white as a sheet, dear."

"Yes," Miss Ferguson said. "Yes, I did." Then it was no trick at all, letting her teeth chatter; they had been waiting for it. "Just no brains," Miss Ferguson told them, and laughed oddly. "I feel chilled through. So I wonder—could I have a little hot soup in my room to-night? Would that be too much trouble for you, Mrs. Bradley? I'm just not hungry."

"Well, now you could," Mrs. Bradley said, rousing herself. "You could, of course, dear; and why couldn't you? I'll send it up right away. I'll speak to Emily about it. But . . ."

Miss Ferguson pushed a button. The door closed. Upstairs, in her room, she huddled herself under a light comforter, in case Proctor should appear with more inquiries. The rain drummed outside, the room got darker and darker with each moment. And presently a certain phrase began repeating itself over and over in her, as another phrase had done earlier that afternoon on the park bench. That man and the child, this one went. That man and the child, that man and the child . . .

The soup came. She drank it, and thanked Emily. Eight o'clock struck softly downstairs; later, nine; then, ten. She was still under the comforter. But at a quarter of eleven she got up, put on her uniform and went down to relieve Proctor.

"Well, well, well. Whom have we here?" Proctor wanted to know, immensely cheerful with the question, since the patient appeared to be a bit more aware and alert tonight. "Why, I do believe that it's our Miss Ferguson," she added brightly, "right on the dot for us, and fresh as a daisy. Now you're going to be in good hands tonight, Mrs. Cannaday, believe you me. Everyone gets along with Miss Ferguson. They just have to. There's something about her, that's all."

And she chattered away, maneuvering Miss Ferguson over to the French writing desk by one of the windows. There her tone changed markedly and at once.

"Fresh as a daisy," she grunted then. "Well, like fun. If you want the truth, Fergy, you look worse than she does, a lot worse. What in the world happened to you this afternoon?"

"Nothing," Miss Ferguson said. "I just got caught in the rain, Proctor. That's all."

"Then let me stay on for you," Proctor whispered. "The old lady's kind of wandering a litttle, she won't realize who's with her. She's been crying all night. Get yourself back to bed for another couple of hours, Fergy. You look awful."

But bed was where Miss Ferguson had just been. Darkness and silence; that man and the child, that man and the child, that man and the child . . .

"Please," she said, again desperately close to that full limit of hers. "I'm all right, I tell you—and I'm not tired a bit, Proctor. Don't fuss so."

Then Proctor marched off huffily, grumbling to herself, and the second night at Ridge Hill began for Miss Ferguson. It proved to be longer and more eventful than the first one. At half past twelve, when the patient was sleeping quietly, with only a low, fretful whine now and again, Mrs. Bradley came up from the main hall with a plate of cookies and a pot of strong coffee.

"I sit down to watch one of them old movies on television," she admitted, while Miss Ferguson was standing out in the corridor with her and drinking the coffee, very grateful for it, too. "And then the first thing I know, I just drop off to sleep over them. But do you know if

Mr. Burden got in yet? I'm not sure whether or not to turn off the terrace light downstairs. Did you hear him come up?"

"No, I didn't," Miss Ferguson told her. "He didn't say where he was going, Mrs. Bradley?"

"Not to me," Mrs. Bradley said. "He's in one of his moods, dear. He's been in it all evening. Then somebody called him about eleven o'clock. They must have picked him up at the gate, too. He walked down there. I wonder who it would have been at that hour?"

Miss Ferguson could have suggested an answer to her. Miss Ferguson did not. "Someone," Katie Stoner had whispered to her that afternoon, "who'd crack your neck for you with his two hands. By God he would!" It was not a comforting thought, and Miss Ferguson did not care to be left alone with it just then. So she glanced in at Mrs. Cannaday, closed the bedroom door partly, and had more coffee.

"I haven't seen him since this afternoon," she said. "Then he gave me a ride home from town. He and Elizabeth."

"Did he?" Mrs. Bradley said. It was the first time they had ever discussed Robert Burden, and she must have felt a curious lack of warmth in the answer she made. She sat down on one of the hall chairs, at any rate, her honest old face clouding up.

"If you only knew how to take him," she said. "But I just don't, dear—and he's been something like eight years in the house now. Ah, well. It all depends on how he happens to feel, you know. I've seen days when there wasn't so much as a civil word to any of us. Not to the child, even."

Miss Ferguson put down her cup. She knew exactly what she had to do with that opening; quite suddenly she had found cunning and unexpected resources within herself.

77

"I noticed that," she said. "I noticed it in the car this afternoon. He doesn't spoil Elizabeth, does he?"

"I suppose it's his way," Mrs. Bradley said, heaving another deep sigh, as if still troubled by the subject. "And I suppose it's the damned money that does it to them. They're just not as close to one another as we are. They live more to themselves, like. But try one of the cookies now. You had nothing at all for yourself but that little sup of hot broth tonight."

"Yes, I will," Miss Ferguson said. "Thank you. His wife died here when little Elizabeth was born, didn't she? Miss Cotter was telling me about it."

"Ah, she did," Mrs. Bradley said, brushing at the side of her black dress now, and nodding heavily. "My poor darling Miss Monica. But then she was never a well girl, you know, and as it happened the baby arrived a bit early, when Dr. McCormick was down in New York at some kind of a medical convention. That's how it was. We had nobody to call in but that drunken old villain of a Dr. Bennett. Even the young Savage boy hadn't started in town yet. There was just no choice."

"I suppose there wasn't," Miss Ferguson murmured, and quite steadily. The cunning had prepared her a little. "And Bennett wasn't a very competent man, Miss Cotter thought."

"Now don't start me," Mrs. Bradley said, grimly shifting herself. "A damned, drunken old reprobate, that's what he was—and may God forgive me for speaking the truth about him. But wasn't I right here in this hall that night, me and the madam, and the madam talking to him? How was the child? she says, when he comes out to tell us about it. Was everything all right? And he shakes his head at the two of us, and shakes it again, and says no, no it wasn't all right—thinking, I suppose, that he had his foot in the door now, and that if he could only make a big enough thing out of it, he might cut the ground from under Dr. McCormick. It was going to be touch and go with Miss Monica, he tells us—and a bit worse than that with the child, unfortunately. Oh, yes, a serious heart defect. Now can you imagine the thing? Why, he put all of us in a mad flutter around here—the whole house. But then Dr. McCormick got back early the next morning, and it was no such thing, Dr. McCormick told us—or not with the child. He said the baby was solid and healthy as a little bull, thank God.—And she was. She was and she is, dear. There's just no question."

There was only one lamp on over near the main stairs. They stood in shadow, save for the faint glow of the bedroom light behind them. At the moment, and despite all those new resources that she had found in herself, Miss Ferguson was rather glad that they did.

"But I imagine you had nurses," she said. "What did they think?"

"I'll tell you who we had," Mrs. Bradley said, again shifting herself, and even more grimly. "One of them practicals from the village; a blackhearted rip of a thing named Katie Stoner. When I think of it . . . But the baby arrived all of a sudden that night, about half past eleven, and there just wasn't enough time to make the proper arrangements. That was it. And the creature we had to call in ran a nursing home those days over on Maple Avenue here—but for young girls, mostly; so you can imagine the kind of a place that she had. It must have been seven or eight o'clock the next morning before we could get hold of a really qualified person."

Miss Ferguson was now standing back against the corridor wall with her hands behind her, her eyes lowered and her expression veiled. She remained in that position. She did not say anything this time.

"A woman of that sort," Mrs. Bradley went on, turning around to her from the hall chair, and extending her right hand impressively. "Think of it. And in full charge of the sickroom, mind you. So it was just in and out with us, for one bit of a look at the child, and that's all. Dr. Bennett's orders. Only imagine the thing!"

She paused a moment, dabbing at one corner of her eye, and then at the other. Miss Ferguson murmured something, perhaps an expression of decent feminine sympathy. It was a little too low for Mrs. Bradley to hear precisely what it was.

"And there we were," Mrs. Bradley continued, her voice shaking the least bit, "me and the madam, and she trying to be quiet and composed about everything, but with her hand trembling on me, and ice cold. 'Now, Mary,' she says. 'Now, Mary.' But you know I just couldn't help it in myself, not when I saw the poor, wizened little infant inside, with that kind of a funny color to it. The light, I imagine. So I ran out into the hall here, and got down on my knees, and crossed myself, and sent up a prayer to St. Michael—and he's never failed me, you know, not for anything like that. Never once in my life, dear.

"Ah, well." She blew her nose softly. "I'm nothing but an old fool, I suppose, but often I go back in my head over it. And I don't say it's St. Michael who did the thing; you can believe what you want, dear. But I'll say this much. I'll say that when I saw it again the next morning you wouldn't have believed that it was the same child. There, now. How else can you explain the thing?"

"I don't know," Miss Ferguson said. She started to move out from the wall suddenly, but then did not. "A heart defect, Mrs. Bradley. Was that it?"

"A very serious heart defect," Mrs. Bradley corrected her, with immense scorn. "When the drunken old fool had no idea of what he was talking about, and couldn't have had. Didn't he admit as much to Dr. McCormick the next morning? But there, dear, I'm afraid I'm upsetting you with all this, or maybe you're not over your chill yet. You're not shaking again, are you?"

"Oh, no," Miss Ferguson said, and in quite a normal tone. "No, no. But where was Mr. Burden when all this was going on? Why didn't he call in somebody from Rhinebeck?"

"I suppose he tried," Mrs. Bradley said. "I don't know. But he didn't get them, however. 'Now go to bed,' he says, after I had got the old madam to lie down finally. 'There's nothing for you to do any more, Mary. You're only in the way here, and I'll call you myself if anything at all happens.' So I went to bed. And when I came down again at seven o'clock the next morning . . .''

Yes, Miss Ferguson told herself, seven o'clock the next morning, hours afterward. But meanwhile? Three people murmuring together in this very corridor: Mrs. Katie Stoner, Dr. William Bennett, Mr. Robert Burden. And there it was, finally. There was a direct eyewitness account of what had happened in this house on the night of August 12, 1957. But what had happened after Mrs. Bradley went up to bed? Who, of the three people involved, was going to admit the truth about that?

Miss Ferguson had no idea. But there was a great deal of time that night to think about it, and she was thinking about it an hour and a half later, when Robert Burden got home. It was getting a little cool then, after the rain, and she had just drawn the curtains at all three of the front windows. She was turning away from them when she heard a car on the drive. She turned back, parted the end draperies a scant inch and looked out.

She saw that man standing down in the gravel turnaround, beside the car. He glanced up first at all three of the bedroom windows over him, satisfied himself that the draperies were in place and said something to the car driver. The driver got out, too, and waddled around to him.

The driver was Katie Stoner.

Once more he glanced up very quickly at the bedroom windows, but once more, through that narrow crack in the draperies, he could not possibly have noticed Miss Ferguson. He was annoyed with the Stoner woman, even so. He gestured angrily at the windows, as if warning her, and then they conferred for another minute or two, heads together, in the dazzling glare of the car headlights.

They appeared to be arguing down there. He moved off suddenly, as if to be done with it, but Katie Stoner persisted. Again they conferred, he with a set, angry expression, right forefinger extended as if to underline and impress whatever point he was making. Finally he lost patience. He walked back to her from the foot of the terrace steps, took hold of her by the front of the glistening blue raincoat she had on and flung her bodily into the car fender.

It was a gesture of brutal physical contempt. He spoke again, soft and menacing this time, right hand still raised. She answered furiously, sprawled back over the car fender, but pointing at him. He slapped her with the back of his hand, and slapped her again, knocking the plump little doll's face left and right, and she scuttled around the car after that with her expression one of shaky rage tempered by a quite obvious physical fear of the man. She got into the car and backed around hurriedly.

She drove off.

Now motionless down there, watching the car, Robert Burden stood with his heavy broad back presented to Miss Ferguson. When the car had vanished around the first turn in the driveway, he dropped his cigarette, put his right foot on it and nodded calmly to himself. It was

82

a slow and deliberate nod, in quite his usual manner. Then he came on up the terrace steps, the thing decided in him now, whatever it was, and switched off the lights behind him.

Miss Ferguson drew back from the window, heart thumping. Then she heard him out on the stairs, and then on the landing. A blind panic hit her. She started in one direction in Mrs. Cannaday's bedroom, then in another, as if what she had previously felt for the man, the instinctive dislike and antagonism, had been only the one-eighth part of the thing itself, the over-the-surface part.

But it was all right, very fortunately for her. Perhaps he remembered his reception by Miss Ferguson last night at this hour, or perhaps he was still broodingly preoccupied by that conversation of his with Katie Stoner. He walked past out in the hall, at any rate, and his bedroom door opened and closed quietly. After which nothing else happened that night; but nothing had to. Water hummed in the next room, and hummed again. Then silence . . .

¶SIX

THERE WAS a phone on the bedside table near Mrs. Cannaday; but there was another one, with the necessary privacy to it, in a tiny reception room down in the front hall. Ellen used that one to call Lucy the next morning. It was five minutes past seven; Miss Cotter had just taken over with the patient upstairs; and at this hour, of course, there was no difficulty in getting Lucy. She was still in bed.

"What?" she said, and then yawned drowsily. "Well, for Pete's sake! You certainly called early enough. What's the matter up there? Anything happen to the old lady last night?"

"No," Ellen said. "Not that." But it had been a rather long night for her after two o'clock, much time to think; and now, as a result of that thinking, she knew exactly what it was necessary for her to do. There were new and rather important things in her. She felt altogether composed. "It's something else," she said. "I went over to Maple Avenue yesterday afternoon, and I saw Katie Stoner. You remember her, don't you?"

The bed creaked suddenly, and stopped creaking. Perhaps two or three seconds ticked off.

"So that's it," Lucy announced then. A certain relationship had been established between them over the years—cool and unquestioned authority on her part, docile submission on Ellen's. She must have counted on that. "Well, I should have known," she snapped crisply. "And I suppose I did know. You just couldn't wait to get over there, could you?"

"Perhaps not," Ellen agreed. It seemed to be the first test now, with Lucy, and she could not feel that she was wavering in any way; so the new things in her, whatever they were, appeared to be healthy and dependable things. "But we can talk about that tonight," she went on. "It's why I'm calling you. Do you think you could leave the shop a bit early this afternoon, and drive up here? It's pretty important."

There followed another pause, very noticeably longer than the first one.

"Now just a minute," Lucy said then, but not quite so snappishly. "I'll do no such thing, and I'm afraid I don't care very much for the tone you're using to me. Didn't I warn you? Didn't I tell you how you'd begin tormenting yourself up there all over again? Didn't I?"

"Yes, you did," Ellen said, still calm. "You warned me, all right—and maybe I'm beginning to understand why, too. But I'd like you to meet me in the Cortlandt Arms tonight, in the dining room; that's the little hotel

85

in town. Could you make it by seven o'clock, do you think?"

There was another creak from the bed. She must have sat up quickly.

"Why, you're crazy," Lucy said. "You're talking like . . . Now look. I can't even imagine what that woman told you up there; what she could have told you. But if you think—"

"Can't you imagine?" Ellen put in quietly. "Can't you, Lucy? Can't you try, even?"

Silence this time, with an odd suggestion of blind panic in it.

"But we can discuss that tonight," Ellen told her. "What she said to me. I'll be waiting for you. Seven o'clock, Lucy. The Cortlandt Arms dining room."

And she hung up, the point of no return dropping further and further behind now, with each minute. The decision had finally been made—to learn the truth; there was a feeling of calm, fatalistic relief about it; and so she had breakfast with Mrs. Bradley, and a good breakfast. Later, upstairs again, she contrived another brief chat with Miss Cotter in the second-floor corridor.

"They're fixing Mr. Burden's tray," she began casually. "He just rang. Does he usually stop by to see Mrs. Cannaday about this time?"

"Oh, yes," Miss Cotter said. "Very faithful; and of course very concerned, you know. Very." She tittered softly, and glanced around at that other bedroom. "Not that you can blame him, I suppose. He's been waiting a long time."

"Waiting?" Ellen repeated. It seemed that there was no effort of cunning duplicity beyond her any more, not against him, and so she permitted herself to frown slightly at Miss Cotter, as though puzzled. "Waiting for what?" she said. "I don't follow."

Miss Cotter moved a step closer to her, small gray head jerking mysteriously.

86

"Why, for the old lady to go," she whispered, poking at Ellen with a sharp, sly forefinger. "What else? Can't you see that he's got his eyes on the money, girl—the trust fund that old Colonel Cannaday set up just before he died twenty years ago? Don't tell me about that, thank you. Because the life income was to go to Mrs. Cannaday for as long as she lived; then to Miss Monica; and then outright to Miss Monica's children, if she had any. And if she hadn't—well, everything to charity, then; every red cent. That's the way they do, usually, through three generations like that; because they can't let it go on year after year. There has to be an end sometime. That's the law. And that's why he wanted a child, you know. Why, he wasn't even a member of the family when old Colonel Cannaday passed on. So there was no provision for him. He'd get nothing at all, otherwise."

It became necessary for Ellen to steady herself then, but just a little. What she showed to Miss Cotter functioned quite automatically, meanwhile. She put on a cool, skeptical smile for her. She shook her head.

"Well, I suppose that might be the rumor," she said. "The local gossip around here. But no one can actually know about that, can they? I don't see how they could, Miss Cotter."

"Maybe you don't," Miss Cotter said, bridling up immediately. "Because how could you, girl? But I do. Oh, yes. Don't forget that it was old lawyer Morrell in town who drew up the whole business that time—Arthur Morrell; and don't forget that there was someone who had to type it out for him. I mention no names, remember. But if the thing was reported to me in strict confidence, then what would you say? Eh? So don't bother to tell me, girl. There's no need. I happen to know, thank you."

It was apparently a favorite and altogether complacent statement of hers. Holy Writ had been attested again; and so she adjusted her cap, smirked wisely at Ellen and marched back into Mrs. Cannaday's bedroom. It was a fine, sunny morning outside. The river sparkled. The fresh dark green of the lawn was still dew wet, and Miss Elizabeth Burden of Ridge Hill, bouncing a rubber ball on the side terrace, was at the same time trying to hop on one leg through a complicated design of chalked boxes.

So, Ellen reflected slowly. There was no question any more as to why a legal succession had been very much wanted around here. It had been necessary for Monica Cannaday to have a child; and it had been even more necessary that the child outlive both mother and grandmother. The whole thing was capable of standing by itself now. Everything to the child; nothing to him. And who was the father of the child—or accepted as such? Who, when Mrs. Cannaday died, would quite simply and naturally be appointed the child's guardian?

She went up to her room. And there was even further relief in having satisfied herself of the truth now. Normal physical reactions took over in her. She felt healthily tired after her night. "I'm going straight to bed," she informed Proctor. "And don't wake me when you come up, either. I don't care what time it is. Let me sleep."

So Proctor did not wake her. She slept hour after hour and woke sound and refreshed at twenty minutes of four that afternoon. She got up then, showered, and brushed her teeth. She had a sandwich and a glass of milk downstairs, returned to her room afterward and went over the whole thing, step by step, in one final checkup.

Did it still hang together for her? It certainly appeared to do so. Yesterday afternoon, for instance, she had paid her visit to Katie Stoner; and last night, very late last night, there had been a secret and urgent conference between that woman and Robert Burden. Why? But the reason was obvious. Katie Stoner must have

88

warned him that Mrs. John Franklin had reappeared suddenly and unexpectedly, after seven years; and she must have wanted to discuss with him, as the first item on the agenda, what precise steps should be taken if and when any further inquiries were made over at 214 Maple Avenue.

That was the reasonable supposition, in any event. There was a great deal at stake here—perhaps ten or twenty million dollars for Robert Burden, and in all likelihood a very comfortable monthly income, so long as she kept her mouth shut, for the Stoner woman. The child could be traced to her, but no further, so Robert Burden was quite safe yet. And that could have been what they had quarreled about. She might have demanded guaranteed protection from him, but he must have pointed out that the only thing for Katie Stoner to do was to admit nothing, no matter what happened.

And yet, despite their bitter differences of last night, they each had a strong interest in making sure that the inquiries were not persisted in. Then what might they attempt to do, either alone or cooperating with one another, in order to protect themselves? At the moment, fortunately, neither of them could have even the least suspicion that the new night nurse at Ridge Hill was the same girl who had called on Katie Stoner yesterday afternoon. But suppose they found out about that? Then to crack her neck for her might be a quite literal warning, everything considered. Very simple, from the Stoner-Burden viewpoint. Get rid of the mother, and the threat of all further investigation would be permanently avoided. And right there lay the risk she had to accept, if either of them ever discovered who Miss Ferguson really was. But how did she feel about accepting it? Was she still altogether calm and composed? Were all those new things still steady and determined in her?

Apparently not. Huddled up in one corner of her bedroom window, and remembering with painful vividness the way in which he had handled Katie Stoner last night, she felt herself a bit cold and shaky again. He could be a savage and dangerous man, when sufficiently provoked, at any rate. He had proved it a few hours ago. And how very simple it would be, during the long hours alone every night with Mrs. Cannaday, for Robert Burden to slip quietly into the room, to get behind her on some pretext, and to use those two hands of his in the prescribed manner. Then poor Miss Ferguson would be found at the foot of the hall steps the next morning, and everything would explain itself in the most natural and convincing manner. A bit of loose rug on the landing, a glass or a coffee cup lying smashed to bits on the floor beside her; an odd, very ugly twist of her neck against the banister post.

"So of course you can see what happened," one of the police officers from town would explain helpfully to him. "I guess she was going down to the kitchen for a cup of coffee, and she must have tripped. Notice that little tear in the rug, Mr. Burden? Terrible thing, all right. Never knew what happened to her."

"I'm afraid so," Mr. Burden would agree sadly with him. "Yes, indeed. Terrible thing, Joe . . ." or Fred or Harry, whatever the name was. He knew them. They knew him. Mr. Burden of Ridge Hill? There would be no difficulty at all there. At the moment, Miss Ferguson might be safe enough, as two separate and distinct persons here: that nice, stupid Miss Ferguson to Robert Burden, and the child's mother to Katie Stoner. But let the connection be established, and what would happen to Miss Ferguson after that?

She shivered a bit, becoming aware that it was necessary to accustom oneself in slow stages to the threat of physical violence, finding her reaction to it an emotional reaction, and not a calm and intelligent one. It was a very warm summer afternoon outside—and yet, suddenly, not warm enough for Miss Ferguson. But of course that was very stupid. He wouldn't dare. And even to think that he would . . .

Someone rapped on the hall door behind her, softly, carefully. Miss Ferguson spun around to it, a bit startled, and saw what she looked like in the mirror opposite. Her expression was tense and strained, her eyes wide, her lips parted. There came another soft rap.

She got up then, watching that other Miss Ferguson, the one facing her from the mirror, with obviously harried uncertainty. But what was the matter with her? There were any number of people within call. There was Proctor downstairs, and Mrs. Bradley. It was broad daylight. She collected herself, smoothed her hair hurriedly and opened the hall door.

"Hi," the someone outside said; little Elizabeth Burden. She was dressed now in jodhpurs, a white blouse and a red riding cap, as Miss Ferguson had first seen her the other afternoon, but she still had that air of cool adult detachment about her. "Miss Proctor thought you might like to go for a ride," she added carefully, as if to make sure first of all that so much was altogether understood between them—that the idea was Miss Proctor's, and not hers. "She said it was just a lovely afternoon for one. Would you?"

"Come inside a moment," Miss Ferguson told her. But she felt foolishly confused yet; the notion she had was that things were beginning to crowd in around her before she was quite ready for them. It seemed to her that she was in two places at once, and had better decide between them—in the room here with little Elizabeth Burden, and also on the landing outside Mrs. Cannaday's room, looking down at a broken and crumpled body that lay motionless at the foot of the hall stairs.

91

"Come in," she repeated, even the words ringing a bit oddly to her. "Sit down, Elizabeth."

"Thank you," Miss Elizabeth Burden said. One of the trim little Scotch maids whisked past, with some clean towels over her arm; somewhere else a vacuum cleaner hummed drowsily. Miss Ferguson sat down also, not yet in full physical control of herself. It was noticed.

"What's the matter?" Elizabeth asked curiously. "You look funny."

"I'm afraid I do," Miss Ferguson said, admitting part of the truth in order to smooth out the much more important part. "I just woke up, Elizabeth. Where do you go on your rides?"

"Oh, anywhere," Elizabeth shrugged carelessly. But Miss Ferguson had already noticed that this was usually the line of defense with her, first the air of indifferent detachment from other people, quite obviously his air; and then, if conditions warranted, a slow, guarded relaxation of manner. The conditions warranted it now, it appeared. She bounced up and down on the bed, as though testing, and pushed a lock of dark brown hair under her cap. She eyed Miss Ferguson.

"Did you ride one of those white horses in a circus?" she asked. "Did you, really? That's what Miss Proctor says."

"Well, no. Not really," Miss Ferguson admitted. There were mints on the dresser. She offered them. "I don't think I'd believe everything that Miss Proctor told me. She teases a lot."

"Oh, I don't mind," Elizabeth said. "It's all right. Do you snore?"

Miss Ferguson managed to smile a bit more genuinely this time.

"Now there's a question," she said. "I don't know, actually. But I hope not."

"You do?" Elizabeth said. The admission must have disappointed her somewhat. She considered it, still holding the mint in her right hand. "Well, I can," she said. "Listen." And she honked high in the nose several times, watching Miss Ferguson intently. "That's how Miss Thornton does," she confided. "I hear her every morning in the next room. She says I just make it up, though. But why would I?"

"Well, of course you wouldn't," Miss Ferguson agreed. It had turned into a quite ordinary summer afternoon again, and she offered another mint and got up. Now she could sit here in this room, she told herself, thinking and thinking about what Mr. Robert Burden might be tempted to do to her under certain circumstances, or she could keep sensibly occupied until she saw Lucy tonight. She made up her mind.

"I think a ride would be very nice," she said. "You wouldn't mind waiting, Elizabeth? I'd have to change."

"Then I'll tell Paddy," Elizabeth said, "and he'll saddle a horse for you. Just come down when you're ready, Miss Ferguson. I'll tell him right now."

The manner and the tone of the voice was still one of cool adult composure. His training again? It seemed, Miss Ferguson thought grimly, to be pretty effective, at any rate. In the car last night the child had been able to return blow for blow, contempt for contempt. Then how could one expect her to react about 214 Maple Avenue?

Sullenly and resentfully, it might be, perhaps even with open hatred, for that matter. Why not? Very soon now she would come to understand what she had lost in Ridge Hill, and what could be offered in place of it by a mother who had abandoned her years ago to someone like Katie Stoner. A child could never conceive of a desertion like that, which meant that she could never understand or forgive it, either. Then what would the mother have gained in the long run, besides the hatred? Anything at all?

Her thoughts came to a curiously addled stop at that

93

point. But still, what was on the other side of the coin, to consider that part? Abandonment again—and this time once and for all to Mr. Robert Burden, and that course of his in the Burden method of child psychology. Yes, no, Miss Ferguson told herself, beginning to feel quietly distracted once more. If only there were a sure, fixed center in all this, and not the constant swinging of a pendulum in her, back and forth. If only she could make up her mind what to do about Maple Avenue, and how to do it!

She dressed in slacks and a light pullover sweater, and went downstairs. Elizabeth was waiting down there. "Now do come on," she cried out impatiently, already mounted on the black-and-white pony. "It's four o'clock. Come on, Miss Ferguson."

So they went on. They rode off on a dirt path into the woods in back, Elizabeth bobbing ahead in order to show things, and certain matters transpired that afternoon between them. They transpired not out of cunning and deliberate leading on this time, as they had a few hours ago with Miss Cotter, and with Mrs. Bradley last night; and yet they transpired, with the line of defense down a bit lower now, and Miss Elizabeth Burden revealing a healthy absorption in herself, in what she did at Ridge Hill, and in the people she did it with, usually.

Very little, it developed then, was done in the company of Mr. Robert Burden. It was Paddy the groom, when his other duties left him free for an hour or two, who rode in the woods with her; it was Miss Thornton who took her to see her friend Barbara Ann; and it was Mrs. Bradley who could be coaxed into reading stories to her at bedtime. Robert Burden was never once mentioned by name, not by either of them, and yet he was present to Miss Ferguson the whole time. He was present most of all, perhaps, when they had stopped to wave down at a passenger train speeding along under them, north to Albany, and when Elizabeth squatted down on her heels then, making determined efforts to split a blade of grass in her fingers, and to whistle through it, the way Paddy could do.

"He teaches me lots of things," she explained to Miss Ferguson. "He's going to show me how to build a trap, even, so I can catch my own rabbit in it. He used to catch them in Ireland all the time. They ate rabbits. I wouldn't eat mine, though, and I wouldn't let anybody else, either."

She tried with another blade, not successfully.

"Oh, double-darn drat," she said. "Why can't I? Do you think Paddy is a drunken, ignorant lout, Miss Ferguson? What does lout mean?"

Something cold and thin touched Miss Ferguson on the back of the neck. The child psychology again? The forcing down under the thumb little by little? The friends she made, the capacities she admired, the tastes she had . . .

"No," Miss Ferguson said. "No, I don't. Who said that, Elizabeth?"

"Oh, someone," Elizabeth said. She smiled to herself, a secret and malicious smile, and blew furiously again. "But I don't care," she added. "I just laugh, that's all. I like Paddy."

And yet the thing had been said to her. By whom? Miss Thornton, whatever her opinion of Paddy, would have been much too refined. It had not been said by Miss Thornton then, and certainly not by Mrs. Bradley. Then who was left? Who would feel it necessary, even at this early age, to bend Miss Elizabeth Burden to his wish, his will, his command? And there might be another reason besides that one. Continued pretense could wear on the nerves year after year, and in the end could wear dangerously thin, it might be. So now and again, when in private, and with no one to hear . . .

"There!" Elizabeth cried, having at last produced a

shrill, sputtery squeak for perhaps a third of a second. "I did that time, didn't I? Now listen. Listen to me, Miss Ferguson. Please listen."

Then Miss Ferguson tried, too, and failed lamentably until the proper instructions had been offered. Their conversation went on, meanwhile. Mrs. Bradley thought she knew a lot about God, it had developed. Did Miss Ferguson?

"No," Miss Ferguson said, not quite sure whether the secret and malicious smile was still facing her, and so watching the broad, sunlit surface of the Hudson under them. "Just a little, perhaps, but not a lot, Elizabeth. Everybody ought to know a little, oughtn't they?"

"Why?" Elizabeth said, with no question at all about the smile this time. "You're silly. You sound like Mrs. Bradley, almost. Mrs. Bradley tells me about heaven all the time. But you know what it is? It's dumb, heaven. There's nobody up there. Mrs. Bradley only thinks that they are. They're just dead."

Which had to be the someone again, Miss Ferguson understood. The someone who could relay, with stupid and cutting sarcasm, the idea of "dumb heaven," from whoever had said it first, to a seven-year-old child; the someone who unburdened himself in that way, year after year, of the galling exasperation that appeared to be growing more and more intolerable to him. The someone had bought her a black-and-white pony, true enough. Good public relations. But under cover of that the training went on, and the earlier the better, of course. Seven years old, eight, nine. Until . . .

"You don't say very much," Elizabeth went on, both arms locked around her knees, while still rocking comfortably. "You just listen to people. I don't. I like to ask questions all the time. And you know what I think?" The brown eyes glittered aside covertly at Miss Ferguson, hard and shiny as dark glass. "I think if someone doesn't like you, then you don't have to like them, either, no matter who they are. Now that's fair, isn't it? Or can you tell that about people, when you're all alone with them, I mean—if they like you or not? I can."

"Perhaps sometimes," Miss Ferguson said. There was a launch out on the river, all white paint and polished brass. It glittered painfully. "Elizabeth," she said. "Elizabeth. That's a very important decision to make. I'd . . . you could be wrong about it. And if you are—"

"No, I'm not," Elizabeth said, rocking again, small face set. "I can tell, Miss Ferguson. I just know."

"Elizabeth . . ." Miss Ferguson began again. She reached over and touched the shoulder nearest to her. It twitched off.

"Now please," Elizabeth said. "Don't do that. You are silly, aren't you? Ha-ha." And she rose then, a small but imperious figure under the red cap, and once more coolly sufficient unto herself. "I don't like it," she said, "and I want to go home now. What do people get silly for? I'm thirsty. Come on."

It was not a great revelation, perhaps, and yet, if in a somewhat obscure manner, it did give Miss Ferguson that one fixed point she had wanted. She never wavered a bit from then on, at any rate. She went up to her room when they got back, Elizabeth skipping away from her in the hall with that shrill and horribly penetrating laugh of hers. But then Miss Ferguson came down at ten minutes before seven, dialed the cab company from the reception-room phone and went to meet Lucy.

¶SEVEN

And Lucy was there, too. Lucy was waiting for her She must have been waiting for some time. There were two or three cigarettes in the ashtray, and an empty martini glass on the table. When she saw Ellen come in she set her lips tightly and picked up the big menu card She offered no greeting of any kind, not a nod, even; so it appeared, for whatever advantage it might offer, that she had determined to let Ellen begin the thing.

Ellen began it.

"I'm very glad you came up," she said evenly. "I hoped you would. But then you had to, didn't you? You know what it's about, of course."

"What it's about!" Lucy repeated. She fussed irritably with her cigarette case, her napkin, her drinking glass. She studied herself in a small mirror, when those other resources ran out, and applied lipstick. "But I knew that last week," she snapped crushingly. "Knowing you. You had to go see that woman, of course. You just couldn't wait, could you? And I told you what would happen the very minute you got up here. You didn't fool anybody. I could see the idea in your head all along."

"Could you?" Ellen said. "That's odd. Because I never intended to see her at all. Not as long as I lived, Lucy."

"Well, of course," Lucy said. There were thin, worn lines in her face, despite the carefully applied makeup; she looked stylishly elegant in a simple white dress and a black belt; and yet the eyes, and a certain thick clumsiness around the mouth, hinted at something miserably furtive and ravaged in her. She made a good attempt to disguise it, however. "Oh, naturally," she added. "I knew that, too. But you did?"

"That's right," Ellen said. The quicker the better, she had decided on the ride in. Why waste any time? That man had possession of the child; that man was training her in a certain way, month after month, for his own reasons; and that man had nine points of the law in back of him. She had the tenth; only the tenth. And what that might mean . . .

She set her teeth delicately, and unfolded the napkin.

"I saw the child," she added then, still evenly. "That's why I wanted to talk to you like this. I saw it yesterday afternoon, Lucy."

"The what?" Lucy said. "What did you say?" She looked up from the menu card, as though unable to credit her own ears; but her hand had begun shaking noticeably. "What child? What are you talking about?

You are in your right mind, I suppose. You realize wha[t] you're saying to me?"

"Oh, yes," Ellen said. There were some people a fe[w] tables away, in the window corner. She kept her voic[e] lowered. "I think so. And I don't want a new dress thi[s] time, Lucy, or a nice little brooch, or some really goo[d] French perfume. I want something you can't pay fo[r] like that. I want the truth. Even Katie Stoner admitte[d] it to me yesterday afternoon. Why can't you?"

"The truth!" Lucy got out scornfully. But the eye[s] betrayed her again; there was the something ravaged i[n] them, wincing back as she crushed out another cigarette having taken barely two puffs at it. "What truth? Wha[t] did she say about me? What could she say? Why, yo[u] must be insane, both of you. And to think that you ever listened to her! When I had everything on my shoulder[s] that time! When I was almost distracted thinking abou[t] what to do. And now you can sit there and talk to m[e] after the way I—"

She must have intended to work on Ellen by tha[t] tone, accusing at once and with the most passionat[e] bitterness. But there was a backfire effect. She worke[d] on herself, rather, and before there was any chance t[o] realize it. Her voice caught. A few broken sobs came. Yet it was not a reaction that touched Ellen in any way. It seemed that there was something cold and cruel i[n] her now; a sharply intent cunning, even against Lucy. Because when one had only the tenth point to coun[t] on . . .

"The way you what?" she demanded, as soon as the[y] had ordered something from a short but overfed blonde waitress. "Go on. Remind me of all the things you di[d] over the years; the money you spent; the presents you gave me. That helped you pay off the child, didn't it? A little, anyway. Then it didn't matter so much the way you'd lied to me—and the way you kept lying. It was all I deserved, probably."

"And what did I deserve?" Lucy whimpered. But she had been forced to concede the tears by this time, which meant that she had been forced to concede everything after them, even the one damning admission—a last feeble attempt at justifying herself. "If you ever bothered to consider that part. Where was the money coming from? You knew I was just getting the shop started. You knew how I had to scrimp and save for every penny there was. So what choice did I have?"

"I couldn't really say," Ellen told her, beginning to feel something oddly familiar about all this, as if it had taken on the flavor of one of their endless discussions years ago, only with Ellen the accuser now, and not the accused. "Yes. You're perfectly right, perhaps. No choice at all. You knew, anyway, what really counted for you: the shop. Every hope was for that; every thought, every ambition. Not for the child. Never once. What did she matter?"

"I did what I had to do," Lucy whimpered again. "I'm not ashamed."

"But if you were," Ellen said, not quite so evenly. "Just a little, Lucy . . ."

The waitress came back. Lucy, keeping her head lowered until after their soup plates had been put down, wiped the corners of her eyes with the big table napkin.

"Then blame me for the whole thing," she whispered tragically; "if that's any comfort for you. And I knew you would, anyway. Maybe that's why I could never tell you about what happened. But how did you act? You remember, don't you? You wouldn't talk sense, even. I tell you there was nothing to do but have it adopted somewhere. Nothing!"

"Perhaps not," Ellen agreed, the first and most important step safely achieved now; the second waiting for her. "I don't know any more. I never did, I suppose. Only . . ." She hesitated a moment; but then she found the necessary hard cruelty in her, to match him. "Only how did you arrange it with Katie Stoner?" she demanded brutally. "Because what it amounted to—you actually sold her the child, didn't you?"

And there must have been something of the same idea in Lucy at that moment. She flinched back a little, crushing the napkin in her right hand.

"Don't you say that!" she commanded shakily. "Don't you ever say it. You make it sound . . . I don't know what you'd call selling it. There were people who were willing to pay all the medical expenses. Was that so terrible? And they were farm people around here; good, decent people. I even went out to see them about it. I just wouldn't do anything, I told her, unless I knew who they were, and unless I satisfied myself that— What's the matter?"

"Farm people?" Ellen said. She felt a little confused suddenly, not following any more. "Wait a minute," she said. "That's not true. That's not true, Lucy. It can't be. What farm people?"

"Why, the Schaefers," Lucy said. And her surprise appeared genuinely unforced this time. She stared back at Ellen, beginning to search her face fearfully. "But I thought you knew. I thought you said Katie Stoner told you. The people who took it. Mr. and Mrs. Frank Schaefer. I remember the name."

But it was still not even faintly comprehensible to Ellen. It seemed that all at once there was something very badly out of connection between them. But what was it? The waitress came back again, to remove their soup plates. Lucy, hurriedly collecting herself, ordered another martini, and then asked the one obvious question.

"Well, now, let me see," the waitress said. "Only Schaefers I knew don't even live in town any more. But he used to run a big chicken farm out on North Pilgrim Road; Frank Schaefer. They moved somewhere. Down to Florida, somebody told me. That the one?"

102

"I'm not sure," Lucy said. She gave Ellen a rather harried glance, to signal her to remain quiet another moment; but it was not necessary. Ellen was still groping for what was meant here; still dumb. "Maybe it is, though," Lucy said. "You wouldn't know if there were any children in the family, would you?"

"Children?" the waitress said. She pondered briefly, not lifting the tray yet. "Well, yes," she said. "Of course. They had one they adopted somewhere. That's right."

"One they adopted," Lucy said. She began to relax then, her point proven; but Ellen, facing her, and making a slight, foolishly denying gesture, seemed to be twisting around slowly and thickly inside herself, without any physical discomfort. She gestured again. Lucy nodded back hurriedly.

"I see," Lucy said. "Boy or girl?"

"Oh, a girl," the waitress said. "And just the prettiest little thing that you ever saw, too. Deborah June, they called her. She'd be maybe six or seven years old by this time. But what did you order again? The lamb chops and the roast beef, wasn't it? Is that right?"

Lucy answered her. But of course with that revelation, and as a matter of plain fact, Lucy was the only Ferguson sister who could possibly have answered her.

"That's right," Lucy said. "Thank you."

"Honey," the plump waitress said, "don't even mention it."

She gave them a lackluster professional smile, hefted the tray into position and went back to the kitchen.

¶EIGHT

It was about a quarter of eight by that time. They remained at their table until eight thirty, Ellen talking quietly, Lucy putting in an occasional brief question; and then finally the whole thing had been explained detail by detail. After it was, Lucy Ferguson sat back, lit another cigarette for herself and nodded grimly. She had turned into the old Lucy little by little, tears forgotten —quick, sharp, practical, shrewdly calculating. For each of them now there was a greater urgency than to assign individual blame and responsibility for what had happened on Maple Avenue seven years ago, and they were

104

beginning to realize the fact. The air had been cleared, and they had become the Ferguson sisters again, that closed, fiercely loyal corporation against the rest of the world; but in particular now, and with everything that had just been explained between them, against Mr. Robert Burden.

"So that's it," Lucy said. "Now I see. I couldn't understand why you got so upset when I mentioned the Schaefers. But I think you're right, Ellie. There is something funny going on here; something darned funny. Let me think a minute."

"I've been thinking about it all week," Ellen admitted painfully. "I thought maybe I was a bit mental at first. But then after I went to see Katie Stoner yesterday—I tell you it happened like that. It did, Lucy. That's why the two of them had to talk it over last night. That's what proved it."

"Proved it to you," Lucy pointed out, "and to me, I guess. But I'd say the only way we can prove it against him is to prove it through Katie Stoner. Wouldn't you agree?"

"If she admits it to us," Ellen said. She had a slight headache again, naggingly persistent. There was no hope in her about Katie Stoner, not even the least hope. "But she won't. She can't, Lucy. She'd be in trouble."

"Can't she?" Lucy said. She rose then, giving another grim nod. "Well, let's just find out. We'll drive over there right now, the two of us—and that creature is going to admit the truth about this if it's the first time in her life that she ever admitted it. Let's see her push me out of that front door tonight. Don't worry, Ellie. Just let her try."

So they drove over to Maple Avenue. No one answered the doorbell, however. There was only a dim lamp on, back in the hall. The garage and the driveway were both empty.

105

"Out somewhere," Lucy announced, after ringing again and then peering inside through the porch window. "Okay. We'll wait, then—and we'll wait until hell freezes, if we have to. But she isn't getting away with this now—and he isn't. Come on. We'll wait in the car."

It was beginning to rain again; thin, drifting mist. The road and the narrow strips of walk flanking it glistened under the one street lamp half a block distant, and lights were on two houses down from Katie Stoner's. Once more, after they had gone back to the car, Lucy considered briefly.

"But it's true about the Schaefers," she insisted to Ellen. "I did go out there that afternoon, and talk to them. And I liked them, too. They were good, solid people. It's the only reason I agreed to the thing. But that doesn't mean Katie Stoner couldn't have made an excuse to them the next morning, after the other business came up. I think she did. I think she probably told them that the baby was stillborn, or that it was deformed, or anything at all. But let's see. Yours was born about three in the afternoon. I was right there in the house with you, and I know. What time was the Burden baby born over at Ridge Hill?"

"Late that night," Ellen said, after thinking back effortfully. "Eleven or eleven thirty, Mrs. Bradley told me."

"Which makes it about right," Lucy decided. "I mean the time schedule. Can't you just see it, Ellie? The three of them knowing perfectly well that the Burden baby was either dead or dying, and that the mother would probably follow it at any minute; and then the three of them whispering together out in the hall, where Mrs. Bradley noticed them. Maybe Katie Stoner got the first brilliant idea. She's certainly quick enough; and there's a good chance, in a town like this, that she knew about the Cannaday trust fund just the way your Miss Cotter knew about it. Those things get around. So let's say that she put out one of those delicate little feelers of hers, with all that lovely money to think about.

" 'But isn't it too bad?' she could have told them. 'A queer old world, all right. That poor little infant in there, with everything she could want waiting for her; and I with the sweetest and dearest little creature—and a girl, too, now that I think of it—born right in my house only a few hours ago. Why, you couldn't tell them apart, I imagine; not for a week yet. But what a difference between them! Because the mother doesn't even want that one, you know. She'd like me to get rid of it, indeed, and no questions asked. Not a one, mind you. I'm to have it adopted somewhere. But who's going to be ready and willing to take it, however . . . Ah, well. That's always the problem, isn't it?'

"So there it was for your Mr. Robert Burden, cards on the table—if he had sense enough to look down at them. And maybe he did. Maybe he jumped at the idea like a starved rat. So he sends Mrs. Bradley to bed, to have a nice clear field for himself, and then he has Bennett put on his big act the next morning with Dr. McCormick. That would be the icing on the cake. All Bennett would have to do would be to admit that he had taken a few drinks, and that he had been a hundred per cent wrong in diagnosing a heart defect. He could even have broken down, and begged McCormick not to tell anyone what a crazy mistake he'd made. That would have finished the thing beautifully. Who was going to suspect anything at all after that?

"And of course I was just as easy to handle as you were; just as credulous. She couldn't tell me that your baby had a heart defect. I knew better. I'd taken care of it that night, even, when she rushed over to Ridge Hill after Bennett called her, and I might have got wise to the thing. So she thought up something else to convince me.

"Here's what she did. When I got up the next morning, she told me that the Schaefers had already taken the baby, and I was stupid enough to believe her. Then she put on the big sympathy act! 'But you know it just wrings my heart,' she told me. 'Now it does, dear—because I can't help thinking of that poor little sister of yours, and the way she's going to plague and torment herself later on, the way they all do. Oh, yes. I've seen them come back year after year, you know, to find out what's happened to it; and what can I do for them? If only—oh, God forgive me!—but if only it had died last night; or if only she believed that it had. There's the merciful thing, and no need to blame herself then for as long as she lived. That other girl in the back room upstairs was a lot luckier. Indeed she was, dear. She's a charity case, you know; I can't refuse them, somehow; and I've got to bury her poor nameless little thing out of my own pocket tomorrow morning, as a matter of fact. You don't think we could maybe keep your sister in bed a few days, and then tell her . . .' But of course I did think. I had a rotten bad conscience, I suppose, with the thing I was doing to you; and I jumped at the idea just the way Robert Burden must have jumped at the other one. Oh, that—that miserable fat bitch! She made fools out of the both of us. It's exactly the way she handled the whole thing."

Ellen had her head back on the seat. She did not answer immediately. But it seemed very probable, she was telling herself. Yes; exactly. Mist sparkled in tiny colorless beads up around the street lamp. It was five minutes past nine now. She sat up wearily.

"But even if it is . . ." she said, the headache a bit worse now. "I didn't mean to blame you before, Lucy. I'm sorry. I ought to have blamed myself, rather. What if I believed you that time because I wanted to believe you? Because I knew it was the easy way out for me? And maybe I did. I thought about that all yesterday

108

afternoon, too, and all last night. I'm still thinking about it."

"Well, you can just stop!" Lucy almost snapped at her, with sudden and surprising vehemence; but then, ever since those few brokenly defiant tears at the hotel an hour ago, it was Lucy who had been the tower of strength for both Ferguson sisters. "You didn't suspect anything. You couldn't have. And I thought it was with the Schaefers the whole time, only I'd promised not to see it any more, or to tell you that it was alive, even. I thought it was the only sensible thing to do, Ellie, and naturally Katie Stoner figured that I was never going to admit the truth to you. How could I? She had me hooked the minute I consented to the adoption. And yet, if I did tell you eventually, she'd have the death certificate waiting for us in black and white. Infant Franklin. Of course! But who signed the certificate like that? Bennett again. So she used her brains, all right. She isn't a fool, that woman."

"And he isn't," Ellen said, groping clumsily around the vague outlines of another idea that had begun to present itself a few hours ago. "Far from it. And I'm afraid of him now. I mean physically afraid, Lucy. Isn't that silly? But . . . well, Miss Cotter was giving me his family history the other day. It's not good. He comes from an old family, all right, but the way Miss Cotter tells it there's bad blood somewhere. The mother had a mental condition for several years, and he had a brother who shot himself. That rather worries me, Lucy. Do you suppose it means anything?"

"Maybe pure gossip," Lucy soothed her. "Don't scare yourself, Ellie. He knows exactly what he wants. He's proving it."

"Maybe so," Ellen agreed. "Yes. I hope it is gossip. But you don't know what he's like, Lucy. I do. Why was Katie Stoner so afraid of him last night? He can go into a black rage with the snap of a finger, I tell you—and I saw that myself. I even think that he was the one she warned me about. 'Why, he'd crack your neck for you with his two hands,' she said—and I believe her now. So you don't suppose . . . you don't suppose, if we keep pushing this thing, that he'd get it into his head to do physical harm to Elizabeth, do you? He just despises her. I know that. I know it out of her own mouth; by a few things she let slip. I know how he talks to her."

"What?" Lucy said. She stirred uneasily back of the steering wheel, considered the idea and then dismissed it. "Well, no," she said. "I wouldn't fret myself about anything like that. She has to outlive Mrs. Cannaday, remember. She's still his insurance policy."

"I mean when Mrs. Cannaday dies," Ellen said, facing it then; having to face it. "And she really can't live very much longer, with the condition she's in. That's what worries me."

"But a seven-year-old child," Lucy protested. "No. You'll just worry yourself sick. He's got everything in his favor now. He can fight us legally all the way down the line with the most expensive lawyers in the whole country, and he will. Don't fool yourself. He'll claim that it's all a blackmailing scheme by Katie Stoner, probably. And with the reputation she has around here . . . But what's the time, Ellie? When do you have to get back to the house?"

It was half past nine. They waited a while longer, still talking together in low tones, but Katie Stoner did not appear. Finally they gave up.

"But maybe it's just as well," Lucy suggested. "Why warn him again? Because that woman would call him right away, naturally. I wonder if Bennett would admit the thing. She seems a little worried about him, doesn't she?"

"She thought that he sent me," Ellen remembered. "Yes. She accused him of it."

110

"Then let's check on the good doctor," Lucy said. "And on the Schaefers. That's the first angle to straighten out. So suppose I stay over tonight, and ask a few questions around town tomorrow? Then we'd have some idea of the ground under us. Do you think I could get a room at the hotel tonight?"

They drove back to the Cortlandt Arms, inquired at the desk in the lobby and got the room. They did not go up to it, however. It was 10:35 now, with barely enough time for Ellen to get back and relieve Proctor at eleven o'clock.

"And I suppose if you feel anyway up to it," Lucy suggested again, "the sensible thing to do is to stay on in that house and keep your eyes open. You never know. Something pretty important might turn up. You're not that much afraid of him, are you?"

"I wish I knew," Ellen said. She smiled clumsily. "But I've got to go back tonight, anyway. They expect me. Mrs. Cannaday could go into shock any minute."

"Then go back," Lucy said, squeezing her wrist encouragingly. "He won't try anything. He doesn't know who you are, even. And tomorrow morning I'll talk to that fat waitress again. But if you want my honest opinion, Ellie, I think we're going to need a lot of help for ourselves. And what we're going to need most of all, maybe . . ."

She hesitated a moment, glanced uncertainly at Ellen and made the plunge.

"Well, we're going to need a man," she said. "Someone who can really put the fear of God into Katie Stoner. So how about Tony Quinlan? No, just listen a minute. He could make all the difference with a woman like that. I've got an idea he can be hard as nails when he wants to be. Then why not?"

"If you don't understand why not . . ." Ellen began, speaking with a little difficulty now in the hotel parking lot; and yet, despite herself, having thought of Tony

Quinlan even before Lucy. "No, please. I'd have to tell him the whole thing. And I couldn't. You know I couldn't. I never even told Proctor."

"Well, I don't know," Lucy said, getting irritably impatient with her. "He's a doctor, isn't he? And I think he'd have a pretty sensible perspective on something that happened to you when you were a muleheaded kid seventeen years old. Stop thinking about yourself as a five-dollar call girl, for heaven's sake. That man's head over heels in love with you. Why not give him the chance to prove that he is?"

"No," Ellen said. She got into the car, feeling almost desperately trapped by the idea; but of course Lucy followed. The fine light rain was still falling. They backed around.

"Not even to help that child?" Lucy demanded then. "Think it over a minute. He might surprise you."

"If I thought it could . . ." Ellen said, looking blindly away out of the side window. "I don't know. Give me a little time, Lucy. Let's see what happens. But he called me the girl from the Frozen North the other night. He had the idea I picked up some gossip about him and one of the staff nurses. That's almost funny, isn't it?"

"Well, maybe you are," Lucy said. "You've just never forgiven yourself. But I like him. And I think if he's any kind of a man . . . Give him the chance, Ellie. You'll lose him, anyway, if you keep acting like this. Or do you want to lose him? Is that the idea—to keep punishing and punishing youself?"

They turned right on Main Street—dark store windows, a few street lights, black, empty sidewalks. Yes, Ellen found herself reflecting numbly; give him a chance. Tell him everything about 214 Maple Avenue; what preceded it, what followed it. Explain in detail about the girl from the Frozen North. She closed her eyes and kept them closed until they had turned right again on the Ridge Hill driveway.

"But maybe it's better not to," Lucy said, when they stopped there on the circular turnaround. "Maybe you know a little more about Tony Quinlan than I do. I won't try to advise you again . . ." and now even Lucy had begun to look a bit haggard in the faint glow from the dashboard lights. "But you have one consolation, anyway," she added, her voice wobbling the least bit. "You had no idea what was going on seven years ago. Well, I did. I let myself believe that woman, when I'd have done anything for you, Ellie; anything I could. Only what I did do . . ."

She got out her handkerchief again. Then, with neither of them seeming to make the first move toward it, they kissed quickly. Lucy used the handkerchief.

"Don't pay any attention to me," she said, apparently somewhat put out with herself. "I'm just a fool. But I'm glad you know. I'm glad it's out, Ellie. It was kind of hard to live with for me, too. Don't think it wasn't. So the truth helped, didn't it? And maybe, if you can tell Tony the way it happened to you . . . I think it would be a lot better for you, that's all. It's going to be spread over the front pages, anyway, a thing like this. And he'll know then, won't he?"

It was plain truth again; and again Ellen found herself helplessly shrinking away from it. She groped back of her for the door handle.

"Give me time," she said. "Let me think about it tonight, Lucy."

"Of course," Lucy said. "Do whatever you decide, Ellie. But you be careful in there. And call me noontime tomorrow, at the hotel. I might have news."

They kissed hurriedly again; then she drove off. It was only then, after Ellen had turned around from the driveway, that she saw a strange black car near the front steps, with a doctor's insignia on the license plate. There were a good many lights on in the house, too, upstairs and down, and she had a glimpse of Proctor whisking around in Mrs. Cannaday's room with a white wash-basin. Trouble?

It appeared so. The front hall, though quiet and deserted, was brilliant with light, and upstairs Miss Thornton and the two little Scotch maids huddled together, looking white and scared. Mrs. Bradley stood off to herself by the big grandfather's clock back on the landing. She was crying quietly.

"Half an hour ago," she whispered to Ellen. "I was just coming up to say good night to her, and Miss Proctor ran out. Now Dr. McCormick's in there. But she's very bad, I'm afraid; she can't breathe right. Listen to her."

Ellen moved down a little, toward the bedroom. Then she could hear a loud, choked gasping from inside, quite loud enough to be heard out in the corridor. It came again. It came faster and faster, with even more effort. It kept coming. Proctor was inside by the bed, standing beside a stocky, gray-haired man who was obviously Dr. McCormick. She was still holding the basin.

"They just gave her some kind of injection," Mrs. Bradley whispered again, drawing close fearfully. "Five minutes ago. But it didn't rouse her. And Mr. Burden is out somewhere. I can't reach him. I've tried every place I can think of, but he's not there. It's just no use."

And she began weeping again. Ellen got her to sit down, and murmured to her. She quieted a bit. Then Ellen ran upstairs, got into her uniform and came down again. At the same moment, Proctor appeared with another bowlful of cracked ice from the kitchen refrigerator.

"I think it's pretty bad this time," she explained hurriedly. "She kind of slipped off on me all of a sudden, so

I called McCormick. He can't rouse her, though. She must have had a lot more internal bleeding. I'm glad you're here, Fergy. Get the maids and that ape Thornton into their rooms, and then come in and slip off her gown for me, will you? We're trying an alcohol sponge. Her temperature's way up."

But the alcohol sponge did not help any more than the caffeine injection. Mrs. Cannaday lay on her back, eyes closed, face darkly flushed, mouth open. She would be quiet for a time, so quiet that it was difficult to say whether she was still breathing; then she would gasp suddenly, and gasp again, louder and deeper, with the most agonizing physical effort. It went on and on like that for the next hour: the stillness of death for a few seconds, the struggle to breathe again, the stillness once more. A few minutes after twelve o'clock Robert Burden appeared.

Dr. McCormick spoke to him in the hall first. Then he came in. It was his game now, as Miss Cotter would have expressed the thought, and yet he looked noticeably upset to Ellen. He did not speak either to her or to Proctor. He glanced over at the bed, moistening his lips carefully, and rubbing one hand down the side of his light jacket. He started to go out of the room, a bit dazed. He stopped. But concern for Mrs. Cannaday, was it? He seemed bewildered, rather. He might not have known exactly where he stood in the room. He glanced at the big walk-in closet opposite him; at the writing desk over between the windows; at the dresser; and at the bedside table. He moistened his lips again, but without helping the befuddled expression in any way. Finally he saw Ellen, nodded to her and went back into the hall.

At one o'clock Proctor went upstairs, to rest until she might be needed again. At two o'clock, when Ellen left the room briefly for another basin of cracked ice, he was standing over by the end window out in the hall with Mrs. Bradley. There was very little to be done now. They all knew it; and yet, in the way of a small miracle, Mrs. Cannaday's blood pressure rose hopefully about twenty minutes past two. Her breathing also became a little more normal. She appeared to rally. Mercifully she was still unconscious, however.

"And you know what this is," Dr. McCormick murmured. "The last shot in the gun, that's all. It doesn't mean anything, because I still can't get any kind of physical response out of her. You notice?"

He lifted one eyelid, then the other one. The pupils were unequal in size and not balanced. Each of them, in turn, glared up stonily at the bedside lamp. He shook his head.

"I'll talk to Mr. Burden again," he said. "Then I'll go home. There's just nothing else to do for her any more. I think she'll slip off nice and quietly now—or let's hope so. You've got my number, haven't you?"

He left then, and Robert Burden walked down to the front hall with him. A few minutes later Robert Burden came back, murmured to Mrs. Bradley out in the corridor and remained out there, after Mrs. Bradley went downstairs, for about five minutes. She heard him move around several times. Then he came over to the bedroom doorway.

"I've asked Mrs. Bradley to make some coffee," he told her. He still had that appearance of heavy and fuddled strain about him, looking over at the bed first, and after that, just as he had the other time, glancing around dully, as if there was something he expected to see in the room, but did not see. Something he very much wanted, perhaps? Was that it? He smoothed down one side of the ruddy mustache with an irritable and yet rather abstracted gesture; then roused.

"Perhaps you'd see if it's ready," he suggested stolidly.

"Take five minutes for yourself, Miss Ferguson. It might be a pretty long session for you; for both of us. But it's all right. I'll stay in the room with her."

He put it not as a direct order, and yet there was a certain unarguable force in the way he kept watching her afterward from over near the hall doorway. Yet, although heavily patient, he did not appear to be altogether absorbed in Miss Ferguson. Was he absorbed in the something else, then? The something he wanted? That might mean something important to him; and perhaps, by the same token, something important to Miss Ferguson.

She had just wiped Mrs. Cannaday's face gently. Now she put the washcloth and basin down on the bedside table. But why did he want her out of the room for five minutes? To be alone in it with the dying woman, to look for something? The thought gave her a tough, hard quality of nerve against him. He knew what he wanted in here. She did not. But there might be a way in which she could find out: give the man rope.

"Then I will," she said, nodding back quietly at him. "Thank you, Mr. Burden. Just five minutes."

There was a chair over near the fireplace. He sat down in it. She understood that he would be sitting there in exactly the same position, as if he had never stirred from it, when she came back, too. But meanwhile? Her thoughts continued to move quickly and sharply in her, well ordered. They gave her even more cold nerve than a moment ago, and the idea that she might have reached a rather critical point now with Mr. Robert Burden. Then get beyond it, she urged herself—and then the advantage could be all on Miss Ferguson's side, and not on his. *She* knew, after all, what lay between them. There was no chance that *he* could even suspect it yet.

So she gave him the rope. She walked out of the room

117

quietly, turned left in the hall, and then turned right at the stairway, to go down. But she did not go down, not more than three steps. On that level, when it was impossible for her to be seen any more from the doorway to Mrs. Cannaday's bedroom, she pressed back into the wall behind her, flat against it, and then waited.

She waited for twenty seconds to go past, attempting to count them off as accurately as possible. Enough time, then? She decided it was. Robert Burden, after all, had managed only five minutes for himself, and he had a lot of ground to cover in that bedroom. It was ten minutes of three by the big grandfather's clock over her, and there was not a sound anywhere in the house; a deep, beating stillness, rather. Yet she was no longer helplessly in fear of the man. The fear remained in a way, very deep in, but it had become a wary and intelligent thing now, to make her careful; no longer an emotional thing, to cringe back from.

When the twenty seconds had gone by, she did what she had determined to do. Three steps up to the hall; left there; back again on thick carpet, on rubber-soled white shoes, to the door of Mrs. Cannaday's bedroom. She had left it a bit open after her, the least bit. It was still in that position.

But a large part of the room was now concealed from her, even so. She could see the bed, however; the walk-in closet behind it; the dressing table; and the cushioned bench or settee in front of the dressing table. Yet, because of the visual limitation, she could hear Robert Burden before she could see him. He was over at the French writing desk, it appeared. Papers rustled there. A drawer closed. Another one opened.

He appeared now at the foot of the bed, moving with that heavy and yet agile physical quickness of his. And he had changed outwardly in some manner, in his expression. The fuddled strain had given way to a look of

118

dark, almost savagely harried intensity. Now it did not matter what he showed of himself; what he felt and revealed at the moment. He glanced back at the hall door, nevertheless, not as if he were thinking about it, and yet alertly enough to have been aware of any change in position there, even the slightest. And then she was afraid of the man—afraid that his instinct might warn him, if nothing else; there was the flicker of something again weak and traitorous in her. She could not help what she did then. She put the back of her hand over her mouth. She turned her head quickly from him—and of course stupidly. How could that help?

Silence again. She could hear nothing from the room. Her ears ached. Where was he? Coming closer perhaps? And of course moving as quietly and carefully in there as Miss Ferguson had moved in the corridor a moment ago? She forced her head back into position, and it was all right. He was over at the bedside table, no longer facing her.

But he must have wanted something in the bedroom, whatever it was. He opened the table drawer, pawed through it and even moved the basin on top. Yet it was at once evident, in the way he spun around almost immediately, that the something was still safely and securely hidden from him. He moved hurriedly over to the dressing table, and searched there.

Still nothing, apparently. He took thought. The closet? he must have asked himself. He darted over to that, pushing aside the door nearest to him. Dresses, shoes, suits; rows of hatboxes. Where? He stood facing into the closet, his back to her, and smashed his right fist into the dresses. The pantomime was altogether unmistakable. Here! Right in this room; right under his eyes, perhaps. And still . . . He became quiet again, head down, broad shoulders hunched up. Then he moved suddenly, turning back to her side of

119

the room again, to the built-in bookcase, it could have been. And behind Ellen, from the direction of the main stairway, there came slow, heavy footsteps.

She did not know who it was; could not think. There was no time to think. So she ran. But she might not have run quite so noiselessly back toward the stairs as she had come from them two or three minutes ago. She ran as far as the landing, hoping to get at least part of the way down before Robert Burden could see her; but she had no chance. She was trapped on the landing. Mrs. Bradley was already halfway up from the lower floor, carrying a tray with a pot of coffee, and cups and saucers. At the same moment, without turning her head toward him, Ellen became aware that Robert Burden had appeared in the bedroom doorway behind her. He did not say anything at all; did not move, even. He just stood there.

"I thought I'd bring it up to you," Mrs. Bradley said, still plodding on heavily. "I knew you wouldn't want to leave her alone in there. How is she, dear? Any better at all?"

"I'm afraid not," Ellen said. The cold nerve was wanted again, and very much wanted. She got hold of it, somehow. "What's the matter with the elevator?" she said. "I couldn't get it to work. Or didn't I press the right button, Mrs. Bradley?"

She spoke clearly enough for Robert Burden to hear what she said, and to accept the excuse from her, if it appeared at all logical to him. But he gave no sign of what he believed, either way. So she remained where she was, talking to Mrs. Bradley, and accepting a cup of coffee from her. He still stood in the doorway behind her. When she turned finally, as if a little surprised to see him out there, he was looking down at the hall rug, not at her, both hands in his jacket pockets, only the thumbs out. There was no sign of what he believed

120

about the elevator, or what he did not believe. Of course. He was in company again.

And after that it was fair play between them; turnabout. Now he could manage the thing, and without giving her any chance to warn Mrs. Bradley; and he did manage it. There was no opportunity for a furtive gesture, or a quick, guarded whisper. He came down toward them. He looked dull and stolid as ever, again not glancing at her; but he had only to wait like that until Miss Ferguson had finished her coffee. He did wait.

"Would you like some yourself, sir?" Mrs. Bradley inquired drearily. "It's good and hot."

"Yes," he said. "Thank you. I'll have it right here, please."

So Mrs. Bradley set down the tray, and Miss Ferguson had to go back into the bedroom. There was no other choice for her. His voice murmured faintly. Saying what? *"Was there anyone out here in the hall, Mrs. Bradley? I thought I heard someone." "Well, no, sir. Only Miss Ferguson, of course. She got stuck in the elevator. But that's all."* Then something else happened. There came a low, droning whine. He must have walked over to test the elevator. Then he came into the bedroom again. She heard him. She did not turn, however. Perhaps it might be a little better that way, she warned herself; to show nothing.

He closed the hall door after him, very quietly and very carefully. Miss Ferguson still kept her head lowered over the bowl of alcohol and cracked ice on the bedside table, very busy with it. He came up behind her. He stopped. Then he moved deliberately again, very close this time—within touch. He had tested the elevator a moment ago. Now, of course, he was attempting to test Miss Ferguson.

"Past three," he said. Again the slow, deep voice, nothing at all different about it in tone or emphasis. "I told Mrs. Bradley to go up and rest for a while. But there's nothing wrong with that elevator, Miss Ferguson. It worked fine for me. What was the trouble?"

"I don't know," she said, still occupied with the basin. "Perhaps I didn't quite close the gate, Mr. Burden. Nothing happened."

And now the toughness of nerve did help; it was quick enough to suggest almost scornfully that all this was nothing but the Katie Stoner bit all over again. Did she understand that they were alone in this room now, quite alone? Did she understand what could happen if Mr. Robert Burden knew she had deceived him a few minutes ago, and had made a stupid and deliberate attempt to spy on him for some reason? But what reason? That was something he could not suspect yet. So let him think whatever he wanted to think about Miss Ferguson and that elevator; he still couldn't be sure of her. The thought gave her enough cool audacity to face around at him, a Miss Ferguson who wanted a little privacy with the patient now, and had no compunction about asking for it. Did he understand? She moistened the sponge.

"I wonder if you'd mind waiting out in the hall," she said. "For just a few minutes, Mr. Burden. I'll call you."

He gave the slow, vague smile, considering her. He roused himself.

"Of course," he said. "I'm sorry. I'll wait in my room."

But then it might still have been turnabout between them—he out in the corridor this time, to watch whatever Miss Ferguson did just as she had watched him five minutes ago. The thought gave her enough warning. She sponged Mrs. Cannaday, wrapped her in the sheet again and sat down by the bed. About half past three Proctor came down, but there was nothing for her to do, either. He was not in the hall then. His bedroom door was closed; and Miss Ferguson did not bother to call him.

"I might just as well sit up with you," Proctor offered. "I couldn't sleep, anyway. And you're a bit shaky, aren't you? I am, when there's something like this going on."

"Perhaps a bit," Ellen agreed. "Yes. Thanks a lot, Proctor."

So it was better then, much better; two of them. He came back about ten minutes later, saw Proctor in the room, stopped short over by the hall door and murmured to Proctor. After that he stayed in the hall. She could smell his cigarettes.

The end came, the last automatic spasms, about six o'clock. She and Proctor were waiting for it. A gasp from Mrs. Cannaday in the bed; a very slight movement of the hand, the only voluntary movement she had made all night, begun but not finished; then a long, quiet sigh, held thankfully a moment, and then released thankfully. It was all over before Dr. McCormick got there; before Dr. McCormick could be reached by telephone, for the matter.

Afterward, with the bedroom door closed again, they all stood out in the hall rather aimlessly: Miss Ferguson and Miss Proctor, Dr. McCormick, Robert Burden, and Mrs. Bradley again. Proctor had called her. Warm, bright morning sunlight poured in through the stair window, and everything looked fresh and sparkling outside after the rain. There was always, as Ellen knew, a queer sort of relief after long tension, a turn to small physical comforts; and now, each in his own way, they were reacting to that. Stubby little Dr. McCormick was rubbing his right elbow and complaining about a touch of arthritis there lately. Robert Burden was smoking a cigarette. Proctor and Mrs. Bradley were talking together over by the end window.

"But look at me standing here," Mrs. Bradley said, drying her eyes almost briskly, "when there's a good hot breakfast to be got for you girls—and for you, doctor. I'll see about it right now. What would you like?"

"Don't bother for me," Dr. McCormick told her. "I had a police call after I left here. I've been up almost the whole night, Mary."

"Well, a doctor's life," Proctor said. "Oh, the joy of it. What happened? An accident?"

"Suicide," Dr. McCormick replied briefly. "Or it looks like it. Not nice. Not nice at all. I'm bone-tired."

Robert Burden had moved over to the end window. He took a handkerchief out of his pocket and dabbed his lips with it, meanwhile standing in profile to Ellen. There was a slight flicker around his mouth, as of nervous fatigue. He seemed to be conscious of it himself. He dabbed again.

"Ah, to do anything like that to yourself," Mrs. Bradley said, looking deeply troubled. "I suppose there's none of us to realize just how lucky we are. Who was it, doctor? Someone from town?"

"Afraid it was," Dr. McCormick said. "Threw herself into the river from Rocky Point during the night; not far from here. And she must have been alone in the car. There was kind of a muddy place around it, and only her footprints. So . . . She took her keys, the way a lot of them do, walked over to the paved area, and then just . . . You knew her, didn't you? Stoner, the name was. Katie Stoner. The fat woman over on Maple Avenue."

There was a moment during which the announcement seemed nothing at all extraordinary to Ellen. Katie Stoner; the fat woman over on Maple Avenue . . . But then there was another moment, with the full force of the thing finally getting to her, in which she was conscious of that slight flicker again in Robert Burden's expression, under the ruddy, carefully clipped mustache, under the handkerchief.

He was still in profile to all of them. Now, however, after what Dr. McCormick had just said, the flicker did

124

not appear to be nervous fatigue to Ellen. It had become something else. It had become nervous relief, rather. Their eyes touched for a moment. He looked stolid as ever, then. But he was still standing a little apart from her, still with the handkerchief to his lips, when Miss Thornton appeared in a flossy blue bathrobe, wailed aloud when she saw the closed door to Mrs. Cannaday's bedroom and began wringing her hands tragically.

¶NINE

THE FIRST down-river train came through at nine forty-two that morning. Proctor caught it.

"Well, back to the dear old daily bread," she remarked cheerfully when the taxi driver had deposited her two big suitcases on the passenger platform. "Only do you think I can stand it this time? Up here was certainly wonderful while it lasted, sweetie. But give me a ring around the end of the week now. Let's do something."

"Yes, let's," Ellen said. It seemed to her that it should be much later than nine forty-two, the few hours since six o'clock having protracted themselves almost end-lessly—the last breakfast at Ridge Hill, the packing up-stairs, and the final good-byes, in the big reception hall, to Elizabeth and Mrs. Bradley. Then Robert Burden had appeared briefly to shake hands, to thank Miss Ferguson and Miss Proctor for what they had done and to present their checks. And to thank them from the bottom of his heart, probably, because of course there would be no one on duty up in Mrs. Cannaday's room from now on, no one to hinder him. Well . . . . She managed to smile at Proctor.

"I only wish there was room in the car," she said. "But you know Lucy. She just hates to be crowded in with three people and a lot of baggage. I'm sorry, Proctor."

It came out as a very feeble excuse, however, and Proctor must have realized that it did. She smiled back gamely.

"Yeah, sure," she said. "Don't worry about it. And don't forget to call Friday or Saturday, sweetie. Let's make it a date."

Lucy was already waiting by that time in the small lobby of the Cortlandt Arms, a phone call having alerted her about eight o'clock from Ridge Hill. But it had been a carefully guarded phone call, from obvious necessity, and so the Ferguson sisters consulted again now in the hotel coffee shop.

"But what do you really think?" Lucy whispered, when she had heard all of the details in regard to Katie Stoner. "Why should she go into a blind panic and drown herself before she knew whether or not you were ever going back to see her again? I don't believe that she did, Ellie. There was simply no reason for it. Did he go out at all last night?"

"Till about twelve o'clock," Ellen said. She wished now that they had gone straight up to the room; the

127

smell of coffee and bacon around her proved a little bothersome. She drank some water. "And Mrs. Bradley told Proctor that she couldn't locate him anywhere. She called all over."

"All over," Lucy said. She pursed her lips for a moment, then nodded tightly. "Well, I don't like that," she went on, "I don't like it at all, Ellie. And we're out of luck about your Dr. Bennett, too. It seems that he died last week in a religious refuge for men near Poughkeepsie. The town paper came out this morning, and I read it in there. So you can see how very convenient Katie Stoner was for Mr. Robert Burden, can't you? He has two down now—and none to go."

They stared at one another. It seemed to Ellen that they stared fearfully, with unmentionable ideas between them.

"And what do you think of that?" Lucy whispered to her, after glancing from side to side to make sure that there was no one else within hearing distance. "Very convenient, wasn't it, the way everything worked out for him about Katie Stoner? What time did they find her?"

"Sometime after three o'clock," Ellen told her. "A patrol car. It could have happened a lot earlier, of course. Dr. McCormick said her watch had stopped at eleven fifteen."

"Then it happened while he was still out." Lucy nodded. "How did he act when you saw him?"

"I thought it was Mrs. Cannaday," Ellen said. But she felt that she was speaking slowly and clumsily now, with marked effort. She attempted to rouse herself. "At first, anyway. Then when I saw him searching the bedroom . . . Maybe we're getting into this thing a little over our heads, Lucy. I don't know what to tell you."

"Well, I think," Lucy whispered, "that he and Katie Stoner could have had a pretty long conference last night. Why not? We were out at her house by about a

128

quarter of nine, and she was gone then. Now suppose that conference ended up in a big quarrel, like the one you saw? He loses his head. He hits her. And then—"

"Don't," Ellen said, in what she thought was a quite normal and reasonable voice. "Don't, Lucy."

But a certain picture had presented itself to her, even so. A quiet road running along the river; a dark, shadowy place, under trees; Robert Burden waiting. Then his whisper to that woman: "Over here. I'm over here, Katie." And Rocky Point must be pretty much what the name implied it to be, a high, lonely outlook over the Hudson, perhaps only a mile or two from Ridge Hill. One would be able to look down from there, straight down, into shallow water. Black hair floating in the water, with a deceptive appearance of grisly movement about it; and of course the plump little doll's face staring up blindly, passing from moonlight to shadow as the clouds came, and then to moonlight again. Not nice, not nice at all, Dr. McCormick had said. That was what had happened to Katie Stoner last night. Then why couldn't something very much like it, but arranged even more cunningly and carefully, happen to the child one of these days, if the occasion demanded it? Let the Ferguson sisters push ahead with this business. Let them push that man beyond his usual cold-blooded caution. And then, certainly . . .

"Lucy," she said, in a low, oddly plaintive tone, almost as young as Elizabeth's had been yesterday afternoon, it seemed to her, "I want to go home now. I want to go home as soon as we can, Lucy. What's the good of all this? What can we prove? Just go upstairs and get your things, will you?"

"Now wait a minute," Lucy said, again glancing around hurriedly. "I know how you feel, Ellie. I know what you're going through at this minute. But you can't protect the child by simply walking away from this

129

thing. It's too late for that. You've thought about blood tests, haven't you?"

"About what?" Ellen said. Clear, hot August sunlight was blazing down out on Main Street; she saw a yellow-and-blue gas truck back into the service station opposite the Cortlandt Arms, and an attendant in a neat gray coverall walk toward it while wiping his hands on a piece of waste paper. All the colors appeared blindingly vivid out there, as though splashed on. Watching them, her eyes ached dully.

"I know the idea you have," Lucy went on, reaching forward and taking hold of Ellen's right wrist for a moment. "You think that Elizabeth will be perfectly safe now if we don't start rocking the boat on him. But the fact is that we've rocked it already, and that he might have plenty to worry about if we can get a court up here to order a blood test. I know they can't prove that a Mr. John Jones is the father of a certain child; but what they could prove, if his type doesn't fit in with Elizabeth's, is that he isn't the father, and that he couldn't be. He's thought of everything else, remember. Then don't you imagine that he might give just a little consideration to that, too?"

"But I don't understand," Ellen complained to her. And she didn't, not at that moment. It was difficult for her to follow what was said now, to arrange it in proper order; the clattering small sounds in the coffee shop seemed raucously loud at one moment, and then very far off from her—a low, infinitely distant rumble.

"Well, you've got to understand," Lucy insisted. "He has full right to the child, and the child has full right to all that money, with Mrs. Cannaday dead. Then why should he even risk the chance of a blood test? Why can't he take her off to Europe or somewhere next week, out of the country, and arrange a nice quiet little accident the way I think he arranged one for Katie Stoner

130

last night? Think about that for a minute. And then decide whether or not you want to— What's the matter? Where are you going?"

"Out there," Ellen said. She rose, the bright colors on Main Street still vividly confusing to her, sharper than life. "I have to face him, Lucy. I have to tell him the truth now. I'm the mother, I'll say. And I demand—"

Again it seemed to her that she was talking in a controlled and perfectly reasonable manner; but perhaps not so. Lucy also got up, at any rate, and took her arm.

"Then all right," Lucy said. "Fine, Ellie. We will go out there, both of us. I promise you. But let's go up to the room for a minute. Let's go someplace where we can really talk about this."

So they went up to the room, Ellen still bothered by that curious thickness of sound at one moment, and after it the almost overpowering hushed stillness. It was a big corner room with twin beds. Lucy got her to lie down on one of them, and murmured quietly. Lucy took off her shoes. Lucy lowered the window shades.

It was a bit better after that. It seemed to Ellen that she began to unwind a little, nerve after nerve; and Lucy kept murmuring to her. They'd go out there right after lunch, Lucy said, about two thirty or three. But just now why didn't Ellen close her eyes for a few minutes? She would certainly need all her wits about her to confront Robert Burden.

"And that will give me a chance to find out about the Schaefers," Lucy added. "I'll find out where they are, and maybe I can even talk to them on the long-distance telephone. That's the sensible way to handle this thing. We've got to be all ready for him. Where's the rush?"

Yes, ready for him, indeed, Ellen thought. She unwound some more, and closed her eyes obediently, discovering then that she was almost completely fagged out after the long physical strain of last night.

131

"That's it," Lucy murmured. "Just lie there for an hour or two, Ellie. You need it. Try to rest a little."

She lay there. She felt herself drifting further and further away, rather thankfully, from the small noises down in the hotel parking lot. At ten minutes before twelve she woke briefly, but Lucy was gone then, and the room was still dusky and peaceful. She drifted off once more. The second time she woke up it was twenty minutes past three, and Lucy was just closing the hall door.

"Now how do you feel?" Lucy asked her. "I thought you were going to pass out on me this morning. You turned white as a sheet down in the coffee shop. But don't get up just yet, will you? I'm going out for a minute or two. Just stay there."

And she left. She could be heard murmuring out in the hall to someone. After that the door opened a second time. It was not Lucy who entered the room then, however. It was Dr. Anthony Quinlan.

He walked over to the foot of the bed, stopped there, and looked down at her with either a scornful or cynically contemptuous smile on his lips. At once she turned her head from him, over toward the street window, and put a hand over her face, as if to indicate that it was only the light bothering her. She said nothing. He didn't. But finally he stirred, jiggling her left foot impatiently, and then keeping his hand on it.

"Might look at me," he began, but with even his tone cool, dry and altogether inscrutable to her. "Might even say hello, Ferguson. I've been driving for two hours. You want a cigarette?"

"No, thank you," she said, now keeping the whole curve of her right arm over her face, not to look at him. But she understood that Lucy must have called him in New York sometime this morning, and that he knew. Of course. Lucy had told him. Her eyes began to fill up helplessly. He stirred again.

132

"Take that arm down," he ordered her. "Come on. You're a big girl, Ferguson. I told you to look at me."

"No," she said. "I don't want to. Leave me alone. Please leave me alone, Tony. I didn't want her to call you. I said . . . Why did she?"

"Well, I suppose that's the first thing we'll have to get clear between us," Dr. Quinlan said, very crisp and professional. "Why she did. Then after that you can do whatever you want, Ferguson. You can wander out into the cold night, maybe, weeping and wailing. I don't care. But you've got to look at me first. Take that arm down!"

A few slow, heavy tears trickled out, under the arm. There seemed nothing in particular to be done about them.

"Don't make it silly," she whispered at him. "Don't, Tony."

"Then don't you," Dr. Quinlan said, still with that cool, cynical smile on his lips. "You've tried to long enough, haven't you? I knew there was something. I knew it. I even told you last Saturday night that—" Then he saw the tears.

"Oh, for God's sake!" he said. He sat down on the bed, giving a strange, hooting laugh this time, and shoving her over to one side like a sack of potatoes. "Well, go on," he ordered then. "You've just made up your mind, haven't you? Why don't you try the whooping hysterics, Ferguson? That's the next step. What are you waiting for?"

"I don't care," she whispered then. All at once the self-pity was not to be borne any longer against that kind of a sarcastic and bullying approach from him. "What do you want me to do? You don't even know what it was like at that time. You couldn't! Nobody does. And he promised me! He said we were going to be married as soon as he finished college that year. And he . . . and he was married. There was a girl from Philadelphia or somewhere. But I should have known all about her, I suppose. Is that what you think?"

"Not quite," Dr. Quinlan said, lighting a cigarette for himself, and then studying the tip of it with his black eyes glittering a little against the room dimness. "I have another idea. All I wish is that your sister Lucy had been big enough, and tough enough, to whale the behind off you when you started carrying on with the local rich boy seven years ago. It's what you needed. So go ahead, if you want to. Cry your eyes out. But don't you expect any sympathy from me, Ferguson. You won't get it."

"I didn't even want it," she said, her voice beginning to wobble desperately. "Not from you, Tony Quinlan. I knew the kind of man that you were, and how much you really cared for me. It's so easy to talk, isn't it? When the way it happened . . ."

The black eyes considered her again, but with no favor. The lips curled.

"Don't tell me," Dr. Quinlan said, still cutting and disagreeable in tone. "It's always the same story, isn't it? And then I get these nice girlish little confidences about twice a month down at the office, Ferguson. I wish to God I could hear a new twist sometime. It happened one mad night, of course—and never again. And even that time he put something into a drink you had, or maybe you fainted. They're the two classical excuses I hear. Which is yours?"

She sat up in the bed, tears forgotten, feeling shamed and furious. Then she began weeping again, and covered her face.

"Now look," Dr. Quinlan said. "You're just not making any impression, Ferguson. That's what they all do when I have to tell them the bad news. It's old-hat. And I liked the girl from the Frozen North a lot better; hell of a lot better. She was honest enough to stand up for what she felt, anyway. She didn't whine and blubber about things, to excuse herself. You know what? You're just making me a little bit sick to the stomach with all this. I thought you knew better."

Again she struggled up in the bed, crouching all the way back against the headboard to avoid even the least physical contact with him. But she had stopped crying again, and for good this time.

"What I knew!" she got out passionately, but with the passion directed out of herself now, out at him, although she never suspected the neat and effective manner in which Dr. Quinlan had managed that part till much later. "When I used to cry myself to sleep every night thinking about it, afraid to tell you. But if you imagine that I'm going to do that ever again—"

Dr. Quinlan got up briskly, tossed a pocket handkerchief into her lap and walked over to the hall door.

"Then for God's sakes don't do it again," he told her, and with a little passion on his part. "Promise yourself. The thing happened, that's all. Why go on blubbering about it? Get up out of there and wash your face, Ferguson. You look terrible."

He opened the door, and Lucy came in.

"Everything settled now?" Lucy demanded, after a sharp critical inspection of both of them. "I was going to give you most of the afternoon with her, Tony, at a minimum. How did you work it?"

"She'll find out," Dr. Quinlan said, the eyes glittering again. "She'll find out a lot of things. And the first thing is that she isn't going to carry on any more the way she tried to carry on just now. Not with me."

The self-pity came back then; she felt that they were both against her. So she wailed aloud, ran into the bathroom from them and remembered in there that such was an old childhood habit—to lock herself off from people when even the least correction had been attempted. As

135

soon as that idea came to her, she washed her face angrily, in cold water, and managed to compose herself somehow or other. A minute or two later she came out of the bathroom, all shaky dignity then, and found them talking together over by one of the front windows. Lucy turned.

"Well, I found out about the Schaefers," she announced. "They got Deborah June from a church agency, and they got her in the spring of 1959. So that doesn't leave anything very much for us but Miss Elizabeth Burden of Ridge Hill, does it?"

"Come over here," Dr. Quinlan ordered, still calmly menacing. "Right here, Ferguson. Sit down."

But she defied him there, anyway. She sat on the bed, hands in lap, eyes lowered with an expression of sulky refusal.

Lucy sighed.

"See what I mean?" she demanded. "Just mule-stubborn. And if you knew her at seventeen, Tony . . . well, Aunt Eleanor couldn't handle her. I couldn't. She knew it all."

"Well, naturally," Dr. Quinlan said. "Or everything but how to take care of herself. I wonder if she's had the brains to learn anything since, Lucy. Think she has?"

"Hard to say," Lucy admitted, "when she starts acting like this, anyway. But I hand-printed an anonymous note for the police an hour ago, and then mailed it. They might just check up on Mr. Robert Burden, I told them. It could be that he knows a little more than anyone suspects about Katie Stoner. I had to do something, Tony. I'm still positive he disposed of that woman in cold blood."

"Maybe you are," Dr. Quinlan said. "And maybe I am, or just about. But we've got to consider that there's still no direct proof against the man. You only poked the beehive, that's all."

136

"I know," Lucy said. "But I just couldn't help it. And the note might be just wacky enough for them to start checking his movements last night."

Dr. Quinlan came over to the bed, sat down on it beside Ellen and lit a cigarette thoughtfully.

"I wish I could get a chance to size him up in the flesh," he remarked. "Then I'd feel a bit more comfortable about passing out all this advice to you girls. The way it is now, though, I suppose the best thing is to slip him the ether before he knows that we're anywhere around, Ferguson. Then we'll operate."

"How about the blood tests?" Lucy asked him. "Would they help?"

"Perhaps they would," Dr. Quinlan agreed. "If they turned out in the right way. On the other hand, if all they show is that he could still be the child's father, then you'd be handing her over to him on a silver platter. You better get a lawyer, Ferguson, the best you can find, and see what he thinks. And then we ought to check up on this Dr. Bennett, too. What was his angle?"

"But we can't," Lucy pointed out. "I thought I told you. He died last week."

"You did tell me," he agreed again. "But Katie Stoner thought he was the one who got in touch with you girls. Why was that? I see something a little peculiar there. You ought to check up on him, Ferguson. It can't hurt. And the sooner the better."

"You," Ellen noticed miserably, not "we" this time. So Dr. Quinlan might intend to go just so far in this thing, but no further. Of course. Common human decency. Well . . . She kept her eyes lowered.

"Then I'll go down there this afternoon," she said, her throat feeling a bit dry and swollen. "I'll drive your car, Lucy."

"What?" Dr. Quinlan said. He blinked over at her. "Oh, for God's sake," he said, a favorite exclamation of his. "I meant I'd drive you myself, Ferguson. Come in out of that blinding snowstorm, why don't you? It must be damn cold out there."

"You said 'you,' " she reminded him miserably. "Not 'us.' So I thought—"

"Oh, stop dramatizing yourself," Lucy put in. "We're trying to talk common sense. And I happen to know Max Benzinger's wife, Tony. She's in the shop four or five times a year for something or other."

"Then see if she can get you an appointment with him," Dr. Quinlan suggested. "It might just happen that he'd go for something like this. It's the offbeat kind of thing that he seems to specialize in. You don't want a criminal lawyer to handle it. Max ought to be just fine."

He stood up.

"And I'd try to set it up for as soon as you can," he added. "So call her right now. But you come along with me, Ferguson—and that's a prescription, remember. You need a little fresh air for yourself. No, no argument now. Get your hat."

This time she obeyed meekly. Yet it was very hot out of doors also. A thin, shimmering haze lay over the parkway, giving it the appearance of flowing black water way ahead, and there were pockets of dead, motionless heat in the low places between hills. They drove silently for a time, passing a car every minute or two. Then Dr. Quinlan glanced over at her, one brow cocked.

"Too bad," Dr. Quinlan said. "Because it certainly looks like we've just about had it, Ferguson, both of us. When are you enrolling yourself in the old-lady's home?"

She turned her head to him, still miserable.

"Had what?" she said.

"Well, you know," Dr. Quinlan said. "You've noticed something about two people riding in a car, haven't you? The older they are, the farther apart they keep in

138

the front seat. So we must be hitting about eighty or eighty-five, I'd say. What do you suppose happened to us?"

"I don't know," she said. There was thick, buttery sunlight over on the hills. She watched it, her eyes feeling swollen and tight in back, a bit strained.

"Then try to find out," Dr. Quinlan said. "Cut it down to forty or forty-two, will you? Grit your teeth."

She remained turned from him.

"Then how about three people?" she said, but not too evenly. "How would they ride? Because I'd have to, this time. I'd want to, Tony. And I understand how you might feel about that. I wouldn't blame you."

"You understand a hell of a lot, don't you?" Dr. Quinlan said, again using the dry, curt tone with her, somewhat annoyed, apparently. "But let me tell you something. Three people could ride in this car without any trouble at all. Plenty of room. Thought you'd be able to tell that much, anyway. You're not very quick, are you?"

"No," she said, her eyes painfully narrowed against the strong sunlight, the back of her head aching from it. "Not any more, or not about her, Tony. But tell me the truth. If you're only being kind—well, I can understand that; I'll even take advantage of it, for her sake. You don't have to promise anything, and you haven't, anyway. So—"

"So what?" Dr. Quinlan growled over at her. "Look here, Ferguson. If all I wanted was to stop off for an hour or two at the next Cozy Corner motel, I'd have made the proposition before this. Then what do you suppose I'm hanging around for? You still think that's all you have on the ball, do you?"

"Maybe you're right," she admitted wretchedly. "Maybe that's the crazy idea I've been carrying around in my head all these years. I don't know. Only if it is anything else, then I'd want you to be sure, Tony. So sure . . . Are you?"

"Well, on second thought," Dr. Quinlan said, uttering that sharp, cynical laugh of his, "no. I'm another type like the fellow that walked out on you—or like your friend Robert Burden, maybe. I just couldn't stand a seven-year-old child around all the time, for God's sake. Is that it?"

"You know what I meant," she said.

"Sure did. Very plain," Dr. Quinlan remarked curtly. "Thanks."

They rode silently again. The tires hummed; hot, thick afternoon air streamed in through the windows, desert dry. She made another attempt.

"If you knew how it was," she said, managing to face him this time. "How it still is, for that matter. I suppose I was the girl from the Frozen North. I am yet, maybe. And that wouldn't be fair to you, would it? That's what I'm thinking about. But if—"

"No, no, no," Dr. Quinlan said, putting out the palm of his right hand toward her, and shaking his head. "My mistake, Ferguson. Sorry. Keep it at eighty-five, if you want to, or push it to ninety. It's your decision, of course."

"There'll come a time," she whispered to him. "Don't worry."

He cocked the eyebrow again.

"Then all right," he said. "Now you're talking. And it'll come sooner than you think, Ferguson. What are you blinking for? You getting sleepy again?"

"Me?" she said, and sat up quickly. "Why, no. No, I'm not."

"Oh, shut up," Dr. Quinlan said. "No, you're not! Ease yourself over here to eighteen, Ferguson, and try the shoulder a minute. See how it fits."

It fitted all right. The first time she woke up after

140

that they were still speeding straight ahead on the parkway. The next time they were off it, and turning in between high iron gates onto a paved drive. There were gray stone buildings ahead of them, and a priest in a white belt and brown robe, tonsured and sandaled in the Franciscan manner, was walking up and down before one of the buildings, reading his breviary. He gave them directions to the information office. They talked there, or Tony did, to a Brother Michael—red hair, a broken and battered Irish face, amazingly contented blue eyes, prizefighter shoulders.

"I see," Brother Michael said. "A friend of yours. Well, we have two buildings for them: one when they come in here, and one when I've managed to straighten them out a bit. Is he still on the booze, do you know?"

"I imagine he was," Dr. Quinlan said. "I understand that he died here last week, Brother. Bennett, the name was."

The blue eyes studied each of them, candidly but shrewdly.

"Ah, yes," Brother Michael said. "And a good, clean death, that he had, God rest the man. But I imagine you'd better see Father Carroll, if it's information you want. Would you come with me, Doctor?"

They vanished inside for perhaps fifteen minutes, while Ellen waited in the car. Then they came out again, and talked another minute or two, and shook hands. Dr. Quinlan ran down the steps.

"Well," he said, when he had them headed out once more for the main road, "here's the story, Ferguson. It seems Bennett wandered in here with a bout of the d.t.'s last spring, and Brother Michael whipped him right into line, as he would anybody, by the looks of him—confession, Communion, the whole works. At the end he was perfectly resigned, Father Carroll told me. Nothing at all on his conscience. A good death."

"Not even the child?" Ellen whispered. "Oh, Tony!"

"Now don't go jumping the gun again," Dr. Quinlan warned her. "He knew he was dying two or three weeks ago, being a doctor, and so he had Father Carroll write out a long letter for him, two letters in fact. One went to Katie Stoner, and one went to Mrs. Frederick A. Cannaday at Ridge Hill. That was the long one. Father Carroll couldn't tell me what was in the letters; that part is all under the seal, of course, under confession—but he and Brother Michael witnessed the letter to Mrs. Cannaday afterward. Now that means something. That makes it a legal document, Ferguson. But where is it?"

She swung hurriedly around in the seat, to face him.

"And Father Carroll told me something else," he went on. "What kind-of-a-looking woman was Katie Stoner—short and fat, with black hair and black eyes?"

Ellen gave him a numb nod.

"To the life," she said. "Why?"

"Because a woman of that description was here yesterday morning. She asked Father Carroll whether Bennett had written to any friends she could get in touch with; she claimed she was a cousin of his, and wanted the address of some people who had been very good to him.

"But you can see what it really was, can't you? Whatever Bennett wrote to her three or four weeks ago, she must have thought he wrote it in one of his drunken fits, and would forget the whole thing the next day. But then you appeared, and she must have decided that he had found out your name and address in some way, and written to you. That was the idea she had all along, remember—that it was Bennett who put you up to the thing. She accused you of it in so many words, didn't she?"

Again Ellen gave him that slow nod.

"The afternoon I went over there," she said. "Yes. I couldn't understand what she was talking about."

"But she could," Dr. Quinlan remarked grimly. "She

142

knew the score. And by that time she was badly worried. Suppose he had written to anybody else about what had happened? So she came down here to find out, and Father Carroll said that when he gave her Mrs. Cannaday's name she had to sit down for a minute. It was quite a shock, of course. Then I imagine she hustled back home right away, and called Burden.

"That could explain their second big conference last night. Why had Bennett written to Mrs. Cannaday, and what had he written? Probably they started blaming each other then for not paying more attention to Bennett. Probably they quarreled about it. And if, given enough provocation, he can be a physically violent man, as you think that he is—well, he might have hit her again, a lot harder than the first night when you saw them together, and he knocked her down. Maybe it happened by pure accident that way, or maybe he decided to finish the job, once he'd started it. I don't imagine we'll ever find out the real story. But then the letter was even more important to him. He had to get it, or he'd find himself tied right in to Katie Stoner.

"But when he got back to Ridge Hill, he discovered that he couldn't get it, not right away, because you and Proctor were in the room, and Mrs. Bradley, and Dr. McCormick. I'd say that was what upset him so much, and why he kept hanging around the hall until he could get you out of the room for five minutes. If he had known about the letter to Mrs. Cannaday before, he'd have searched for it before—and he'd have found it, too, one afternoon when your Miss Cotter was down to lunch, or gabbing away out in the hall. That wouldn't have been much of a trick for the lord of the manor. But he didn't know about it until last night, when Katie Stoner told him. The thing proves itself, wouldn't you say?"

"Of course," Ellen agreed, a bit breathless now. "It does. It's the way it happened, Tony. It all fits!"

143

"Then he'd have looked for it today," Dr. Quinlan said. "When there was nobody in the room. And if he found it— I suppose there's a fireplace somewhere around?"

"In the room," she whispered, her face stricken. "Oh, Tony! Right in the room."

"Easy on," Dr. Quinlan advised, but with a certain softness of tone that indicated the first deep-felt emotion in him. "Just control the puckering string, will you? Father Carroll told me everything that he could, because he knows the whole story, and wants to help all he can; but of course he can't testify for us in court, because what he knows, he knows from Bennett's confession to him, and from what Bennett had him write in the letter. So we've got to get the letter, if it's still around; but if we can't, we'll have to fight Burden through Max Benzinger or somebody else, and fight him like hell. The one thing I can't understand, though, is why Mrs. Cannaday never once mentioned the letter. Any ideas?"

"I think she tried," Ellen said, after forcing herself to think back hurriedly. "She told Tottie Chisholm one night that she wanted to see her lawyer, but that was about two o'clock in the morning, and Chisholm didn't pay any attention to her. Who would have? And even Proctor found it hard to understand what she was talking about; then of course she'd break down, and begin to cry. But she knew about the child, Tony. She told me she did. She knew the truth."

And died with it, Dr. Quinlan told himself grimly. He did not put the idea into words, however. He said other things. He was still saying them, in the most decisive and encouraging manner, when he turned into the parking lot just to one side of the Cortlandt Arms at ten minutes past seven.

144

¶ TEN

BY THAT TIME, Lucy was waiting for them at a corner table in the small coffee shop, but it developed at once that there was no really enheartening news about Max Benzinger, either. He had been in court all day, Lucy told them, he had sounded cranky and tired on the phone, and all he had done was to refer her to a lawyer in Rhinebeck, a friend of his. If they wanted, Lucy said, they could explain everything to the friend in full detail —and then Max Benzinger would decide for himself whether he was interested or not.

"And you called Rhinebeck?" Dr. Quinlan asked.

"Right away," Lucy said. "I made the appointment for eight o'clock tonight. I wasn't sure what time you'd be back here, exactly."

Dr. Quinlan glanced up at the electric clock over the doorway.

"And now it's twenty minutes past seven," he said. "Not much time, is it? We'd just better order a sandwich or something. But how about this Mrs. Bradley, Ferguson? You seem to think she was as close as anyone to the old lady, so perhaps she might have a little information for us about that letter. Do you think you could go out there and ask her tonight?"

"I know she'd help us," Ellen said, making up her mind quickly. "If she could, Tony. She just doesn't like the man. We talked about him one night, and I know that. But she'd do anything for Elizabeth. I'm positive that she would."

"Without honor," Dr. Quinlan murmured, "even in his own country. I see. Let's arrange it like this, then. You go up and rest for an hour or so, while Lucy and I go down and explain matters in Rhinebeck; and after we get back here, which ought to be around nine or nine thirty, I'll drive you out to Ridge Hill, and let you talk to her. That's the best way. I don't want you going out there alone, Ferguson, not any more. I want to be with you."

So they settled it in that way. Lucy ran upstairs after they had their sandwiches, to powder her nose, and he and Ellen walked out to the hotel parking lot. It was still oppressively hot and humid out, even this late. Thunder muttered far off. There were heavy black clouds toward the south, banking up sluggishly.

"And don't forget that rest," Dr. Quinlan ordered. "I mean it. You look pretty well done in, Ferguson."

She summoned up the best possible smile for him.

"I'm all right," she said.

146

"Oh, fine," Dr. Quinlan said. "I know. Just perfect. But you do what you're told, anyway. You hear me?"

"I'll miss you," she put in wanly. "Dr. Quinlan has made a great deal of difference around here. I think without him—"

"Well, naturally," Dr. Quinlan said, uttering that short, cynical laugh of his. "Why not? But let me tell you about the old boy. He's what they mean when they refer to the salt of the earth, Ferguson—and I've known him a long time. You take my word."

He put her head against him, patted lightly, and kissed the top of her left ear lightly, which was a rather marked help at the moment; then Lucy appeared, and they drove off for that eight o'clock appointment in Rhinebeck. Up in the room, Ellen took a cold shower for herself, and changed her clothes. All three of them, Dr. Quinlan had promised earlier—if it only would happen in that way. But if it didn't? If, in the end, there was nothing that even Dr. Quinlan would be able to do about Miss Elizabeth Burden?

She sat over by one of the front windows. But it was very stupid to worry too much about the child, she tried to comfort herself, because Robert Burden must feel perfectly safe and secure now, with everything having worked out for him—the luck of the devil, as Dr. Quinlan had called it in the car earlier. Yet for that man to feel safe and secure now was a good thing, considered objectively. That was the way his nice, stupid Miss Ferguson wanted him to feel—because it meant that little Elizabeth would be safe and secure, also.

He might be a good many things, this Mr. Robert Burden, but he was not a fool, and so he would take no unneccessary risks in this business. Then, too, he had probably been led into the thing little by little. There had been a child nobody wanted, after all; an illegitimate little brat of no consequence to him. Then why not use her? What happened would even be for the brat's benefit, as he saw it. She would attain to a background and position she could never have imagined otherwise, and at the same time, for services rendered to her, Mr. Robert Burden could live in a manner rightfully his by birth and upbringing. Then where was the harm?

It had not been necessary to like the child, however—and he did not like it. Yet, now and again, it had been necessary to pretend natural affection for her, and it was that part which must have become more and more irksome to him. Still, she was getting old enough for school now, of course a very good school, and there would be servants when she was home, and so from now on very few emotional demands on him. Which meant that he could go his own way for the rest of his life—travel, live abroad, marry again, anything. Elizabeth could go hers. And if, in the long run and with a training of that kind, she became as cold, as self-centered and as unfeelingly indifferent to any genuine human warmth or emotion as Robert Burden himself, it was not his concern. She ought to thank him, rather. She would enjoy everything that money could buy. She would be Miss Elizabeth Burden of Ridge Hill. Then how could anyone complain of what he had done, logically? The idea was absurd.

And even the Katie Stoner thing, he might have assured himself, had been only an unfortunate accident last night. Or had it been an accident? Had he planned it step by step, rather? And quite suddenly there came to Ellen the memory of that scene on the terrace, when he had thrown Katie Stoner against the car, and then later, watching the car drive off, had nodded his head after it in that grim, quiet manner. Had that been the moment when he had decided in himself what would have to be done about Katie Stoner? If so, then what happened to her had not been an accident at all. And for the child to be in the power of a man like that, even for one hour . . .

She got up, a little distracted again, and lit one of Lucy's cigarettes. And yet he was well-protected against the Katie Stoner thing, also—if he had found the letter by this time.

The letter . . .

It began nagging at her. But why? What did she know about the letter without knowing it consciously? What could she know? Mrs. Cannaday might never have been permitted to receive it three weeks ago. He could have scrutinized her mail at that time with no trouble; but then, of course, the alarm signals had not been up, and everything had been flowing along with the most tranquil smoothness for him.

And yet, three weeks ago, it came to her, had been when Mrs. Cannaday suffered the bad turn Proctor had mentioned. She had been making a slow but steady recovery, with excellent care; and all at once, as Proctor had described it, there was no more fight in her, no will to live, even. She seemed to have given up completely.

Was that significant?

Perhaps it was, because to be informed with brutal suddenness of what really had happened in Ridge Hill on the night of August 12, 1957, might have had a very bad emotional impact. Bad enough, in her physical condition, to push her over the edge, finally. She had even changed toward the child, because Mrs. Bradley had said that for some time now she couldn't stand having Elizabeth in the same room with her. "Not . . . Monica's," she had wept brokenly, the first night that Miss Ferguson had been on duty with her; and that fact she could have learned only from the letter itself. So it had got through to her, and most certainly. But what had she done with it?

First of all, probably, she might have asked herself whether or not it represented a true statement of fact. She could not know that it did; and of course, until it was proven to the hilt against Robert Burden, she would want no open and immediate scandal. Perhaps, too, she might have had the idea that she would get a little better in time, enough to discuss it sensibly with her lawyer, and with Robert Burden in private.

That must have been the first decision that she made: to check personally on the letter, when she was able to do so, and in the meantime to protect the family from scandal. That was the logical procedure. So she could have deposited the letter in what she considered to be a secure hiding place, close to hand; and that man must have reasoned along precisely similar lines, judging by the hurried and desperate manner in which he had searched her bedroom last night. Yet there was no possible hiding place for the letter, not within Mrs. Cannaday's reach. There was nothing but the bedside table, with the one drawer—a drawer which Robert Burden had examined in about five seconds last night. Not the table, then. On top of it were only pills and medicine bottles, and of course that framed snapshot of little Elizabeth. So . . .

She had been about to reach over for another cigarette. Now she stopped abruptly, hand poised. But wait a moment! The snapshot. Why had Mrs. Cannaday become so upset and excited when it had been moved over to the fireplace mantel? Why had she insisted that it be kept on the bedside table day and night, despite her changed feelings toward the child? The snapshot had stood face up, under glass—but behind it there must be a cardboard or leatherette backing of some sort, to hold it in place. Could the letter have been hidden in there, between snapshot and backing? Was that possible?

She got up a second time from the chair, feeling a

cold prickle along her back, like the tip of a finger drawn there. But why wasn't it possible? Mrs. Cannaday had still been able to use one of her hands at that time, though with some clumsiness. So why couldn't she have used it enough, one afternoon when Emily Cotter was down to lunch, to remove the backing, to slip the letter under it and then to replace the leatherette sheet once more? And then the letter would indeed have been within reach, under direct observation by her at any moment of the day or night, and yet completely protected from anyone else until she could make up her mind about it—and protected most of all, if Miss Ferguson was right about all this, from Mr. Robert Burden.

Perhaps that was the answer. Perhaps Mrs. Cannaday had intended to deal with that man in person, before revealing the letter to any outsider. After all, he was a remote connection of hers, if Miss Cotter was right; she had always had a great fancy for young Robert; and so she might have decided to handle the matter herself, when she had recovered a bit, and handle it secretly and with extreme caution. Only things had not worked out in that way. The shock had been a little too much for her, and all at once she found herself in no condition to question him and get his side of the story, or even to communicate in any sensible or intelligent way with other people. Yet she might still have clung to that one fixed idea: to keep the letter within reach, to keep it hidden from him. And if she had . . .

It was becoming a bit dark in the room. Ellen went over to the wall switch, snapped it on and stood against the door for a moment, still thinking hurriedly. There was, of course, no certainty that she was right in all this; and still, if she was, the letter might be still there. That man had not managed to get hold of it last night, at any rate. There had been neither the time nor the opportunity for him, not with all the people around. Had he

151

found it today, however? He might have, he might not. Yet the one certain thing was that, given enough time, and with only so many objects to examine in that bedroom, he would find it sooner or later for himself—unless, of course, there was someone else who had the nerve and the determination to find it before he did.

And could he have searched for it today, for that matter? There must have been a great many details to settle about Mrs. Cannaday's funeral—and then, too, he might just have been stolid and cautious enough to warn himself that he would still have to be very careful with Mrs. Bradley around, and all the servants. The quiet hours of the night, rather, he might have counseled himself, when there would be no one to see what he was doing, and afterwards to whisper about it. Then why rush anything? He was going to be in full and unquestioned command at Ridge Hill from now on—and he knew what he had to have! There was only one thing he could not suspect, which was that Miss Ferguson knew it, too—and knew exactly where to look for it, where it might be. And all she needed to prove it out for herself was about half a minute alone and unobserved in that bedroom.

Could she manage the thing?

Lucy had left her car keys on the dresser. She snatched them up, slammed the bedroom door after herself and ran down to the parking lot. Where was Tony? Why wasn't he back from Rhinebeck yet? Should she wait? But already the excuse for Mrs. Bradley was taking on plausible outline for her.

"Well, no," she could explain glibly at Ridge Hill. "I didn't go down on the train this morning with Miss Proctor. It's so hot. I'm staying a day or two at the hotel, Mrs. Bradley, and I'm very sorry to disturb you like this. But I wonder if you could let me slip upstairs to Mrs. Cannaday's room? I left my fountain pen on the bedside table, and I thought— Oh, thank you. Thank you very much. No, don't bother to come up with me. Please don't. I know exactly where I laid it down last night. I won't be two minutes."

Or would that man have put the bedroom under lock and key by this time? He was shrewd enough. He would permit no one to walk into that bedroom and discover by pure chance what he had been unable to find during those desperately harried few minutes last night. So perhaps, even if Mrs. Bradley accepted her story . . . But now here she was, another and savagely impatient Miss Ferguson whispered to her, raising doubts for herself out of pure shameful cowardice, and waiting for Tony, when there was only one possible chance for her to find out if the letter was still in Mrs. Cannaday's bedroom. Tomorrow might be too late. Even another hour or two might be too late. But now . . .

After that thought came to her, she hesitated no longer. She ran back into the Cortlandt Arms and left a message with the desk clerk for Dr. Quinlan. Five minutes later, with the first slow drops of rain beginning to fall, she was pulling up in the gravel turnaround at Ridge Hill.

It was now full dark, just a few minutes before nine o'clock, and yet she could see no lights anywhere in the house, upstairs or down, not even in the front hall. What had happened? But again she hesitated only a bare moment. A few raindrops pattered off in the woods behind her as she reached the terrace, and a lemon curl of moon popped out, between angry black clouds, to shine down for a moment against the upper windows of Ridge Hill with a dark, colorless luster.

She rang the bell.

She could hear the chimes inside: slow, mellow. But no one came. In the hall, through one of the glass panes at the side of the front door, she could make out the dim

153

gleam of a fireplace andiron, and the fainter darkness of the big arched window in back, over the stairs. She rang again. After that she remembered the cottage behind the barn, Paddy the groom's cottage. She ran down to the end of the terrace and saw a lighted window from there, and a lighted doorway. Then she saw Paddy himself crossing to her, pipe in mouth, as if he had heard the car a minute ago. The two big Dalmatians were padding silently along behind him.

"I'm here at the front door," she called out. "Isn't there anyone home, Paddy?"

"Ah, there isn't," Paddy said, peering up curiously at her from the edge of the gravel turnaround. "Is that Miss Ferguson? But you see they're burying the old lady down in Virginia tomorrow afternoon, and the whole staff was sent off by car only a few hours ago. It's a mark of respect that Mr. Burden wanted for her. They'll attend the ceremony, Miss. They're all gone."

And very considerate of Mr. Burden, she thought grimly. He had not been only clever enough to lock up the room; he had locked up the whole house.

"So that's it," she said. "I wondered. Well, I forgot my fountain pen this morning; I think perhaps I left it up in Mrs. Cannaday's bedroom. Could you let me inside for just a minute, Paddy?"

"Ah, now, I couldn't," Paddy said, taking the pipe out of his mouth, and then shaking his head regretfully. "I'm sorry, Miss. But I suppose Mr. Burden never thought of the key, not with all the flurry and bustle around here all day—nor I didn't, myself. Could Mrs. Bradley send it to you?"

She hesitated another moment, groping for some kind of reasonable insistence to present itself. None did.

"All right," she said then. "Thanks, Paddy. I'll be in touch with Mrs. Bradley about it. I'll send her my address."

"I would," Paddy said, immensely relieved by the suggestion. "I would indeed, miss. Isn't that the best thing?"

And then he walked over to the car with her, very helpful. So she had to back around in it, wave brightly at him and drive out again to Greenway Road. Once out there, however, she did not drive very far. She slowed down after the first turn, pulled in on an open field off to the right and parked there behind an old wooden shed. Presently, when she thought Paddy would have settled down for the night, she crossed Greenway Road on foot, and started walking up the Ridge Hill driveway.

There was the same light still on in Paddy's cottage. She moved ahead cautiously, even so, the woods in deep shadow now, the rain pattering once more, and dying out once more. Just as she reached the gravel turnaround, Paddy's light winked out.

It came to her as the best possible omen. Never again, she warned herself, would Ridge Hill lie so open and defenseless to her as it did now. She glanced back at all the shadows along the drive, and saw a pale, silent flicker of heat lightning across the river.

She went on, even more cautiously, reached the terrace, and tried one of the tall French windows on that level. No use, however. It was locked tight. Bracing herself against the house wall, she stood awkwardly on one leg, removed her left shoe, and set it in place on one of the small windowpanes. Then there came another good omen. Wind swept noisily through the trees behind her, and under cover of it she smashed in her right elbow against the shoe, full force. Glass tinkled. Using the heel now, she tapped out the edges of the pane so as not to cut herself, slipped her hand through and lifted the catch. A moment afterward, with the window again closed and locked behind her, she was inside.

155

¶ELEVEN

AND SHE COULD remember the room layout in there. It was the place from which she had called Lucy yesterday morning, a small reception room with a mirror opposite, a table and lamp center, and on the right a door out to the front hall.

The door had been left open. She moved for it, though with an uneasy idea that she must not disturb the perfect surrounding stillness in any manner, and the bit of moon reappeared for another moment or so. It shone down at her through the enormous arched window over the stairs, heavy clouds framing it, and vanished abruptly. After that it seemed blacker than before to her, and more oppressive in some way. Another impression came to her of things watching, silent things, things back in the shadows; and it was an impression that tempted her to remain exactly as she was, not a sound or a movement now—to become one of the things herself, as it were, to remain quite silent and quite motionless, as they did. Yet she understood that there was no need for such extreme caution on her part. The house was deserted. And so she managed to edge out into the hall little by little, and found it somewhat better out there, altogether familiar territory to her, not so black.

A long table on her left. Beside it, a chair with broad wooden armrests and a high back, and then, further on, directly ahead, a dark, polished gleam from the oak handrail along the stairs.

The rail guided her. She went up. But then, on each side, the second-floor corridor lay in pitch blackness for Miss Ferguson, and with something oddly disturbing and out of place about it, something wrong. What? She set her teeth, glancing down instinctively at the lower hall under her, hesitated once more—and understood what was wrong. The big grandfather's clock loomed up before her, but loomed silently. Then she remembered the song:

> *Bought on the morn*
> *That the old man was born,*
> *It was always his pleasure and his pride;*
> *But it stopped, short,*
> *Never to go again,*
> *When the old man died.*

Or the old woman, in this case. But it was just that someone had forgotten to wind it today, Miss Ferguson

157

encouraged herself. That was all. And yet from then on, with the lugubrious old tune ringing sadly and distortedly in Miss Ferguson's ears, the things in here appeared to be watching her even more attentively, and from not quite so far back in the shadows, either.

And she had been a hundred per cent right about the bedroom door. Locked, of course. So now what? She took it as a very promising development, however. A locked door to Mrs. Cannaday's room indicated that there was still something to guard inside. An open door, with that man, would have indicated the reverse. Good, then. Still a chance. But how to get in?

She considered quickly. Perhaps it would be possible to enter it from the next bedroom along, from his bedroom. She tried that. No. The nearest window in Mrs. Cannaday's room was at least six feet away from Miss Ferguson even then, and there was no broad, comfortable ledge on which she could balance herself on the way over to it. She took more thought. A way up from the terrace, perhaps? A ladder?

She closed Robert Burden's bedroom window as carefully as she had opened it, reminding herself that there must be a ladder around back somewhere, in one of the outbuildings. But around back would be Paddy's territory. She might be heard, consequently, or sensed. The Dalmatians might prove themselves to be very excellent watchdogs. Then what else offered? An idea came, just one idea. She groped back to the hall.

But the stillness out there had become ominously intent by this time, as if very much aware of Miss Ferguson, and concentrating on her with weak, spiteful malice. *When the old man died* . . . Again she set her teeth. Then the bit of moon came out, as abruptly as it had vanished a few minutes ago, and she could make out hard, black shadows on the second-floor landing—a line of precisely slanted thin strips from the stair railing, and a mass of heavier darkness on her side of the grandfather's clock, where it jutted out from the wall somewhat. Yet, despite the much better visibility offered her, she still felt the darkness as bolder and more aggressive now, even crowding in a little, as if the ways of escape were being slyly and triumphantly cut off against her—doors closing without a sound, windows under guard, bars dropping in place. It was true that she had got into the house five minutes ago, and with no trouble. The awareness had wanted her in. Of course. Would it let her get out, however?

And with that idea she began to feel the awareness as Robert Burden, personally; to feel that she had been deliberately lured here in order to show that man the way he had not been able to discover for himself last night; and to be altogether convinced that he was one of the presences watching her at this moment, knowing everything that she did, and everything that she thought, even. It was not a good feeling. Ellie Ferguson wanted to crouch back helplessly from it, putting one hand over her mouth, but almost at once a calm and efficient alter ego took over—the other Miss Ferguson, quite sensible and composed about such nonsense.

The third floor . . . A skylight up there, so that she could see Mrs. Bradley's bedroom at the head of the stairs, the door to it standing open, the vague white bulk of the bed inside, the darker and heavier bulk of the maple dresser. So, with Miss Ferguson still driving her, she managed to enter the bedroom, to draw down the shades on the two front windows and to risk a light for herself.

The light was necessary. There was something to find in here. So she had to turn on a small boudoir lamp, which gave even Miss Ferguson a rather bad moment. Now, it came to her, she was doing what Robert Burden had been doing in Mrs. Cannaday's bedroom a few hours ago—trying hurriedly, before anyone came, to locate something of the utmost importance. And Miss Ferguson had been watching him then; so perhaps, turnabout once more, he was watching her now.

She even turned her head to the corridor, to look and listen for him; but as soon as she did that, the cool and superior Miss Ferguson lost all patience with her, and whispered scornfully. After that, feeling thankfully numb to have anyone at all take over for her, she followed explicit instructions. She opened one of the dresser drawers, and another one; and in there, between a lilac pincushion and an old-fashioned black leather pocketbook, she found what she wanted—the big key chain, with all the household keys fastened to it, that Mrs. Bradley carried around with her on every work morning.

Then there was no problem at all. Quick, though, Miss Ferguson ordered her, no time to waste on this business. Hurry, hurry, hurry! And she did hurry, almost knocking over the lamp because of it; while downstairs, of course, it was necessary for her to try key after key, fingers jumping and fumbling, before the door to Mrs. Cannaday's bedroom finally swung open.

"And now stand there watching and listening for him," Miss Ferguson whispered furiously again. "Oh, you complete nitwit! The whole house empty, not a sound anywhere, as you know perfectly well, but your silly old heart thumping, and the door wide open for you. And still . . . Well, thank you. Thank you very much, but now close the door after you, just in case. Now the shades. Pull them all down, and then pull the drapes into place. Oh, if I could only do it myself! What are you shaking for? What's the matter with you? The lamp. Turn on the lamp, stupid! You're going to need it, aren't you? And Paddy's all the way around back. He couldn't see anything even if he were still awake in the cottage. Go on!"

160

Again she obeyed numbly. The lamp came on. It showed the bed beside her, stripped down to the mattress as she and Proctor had left it that morning, and looking strangely and unsuitably disordered in such a condition; but she did not really look at the bed. The white washbasin was still in place; so were the medicine bottles; so was the telephone; and so, under the other telephone on the wall, the house telephone with its private connections to the kitchen, to Mrs. Bradley's room, to the garage out back, and to Paddy's cottage, was the framed snapshot.

Now it was facing in toward the bed, as Mrs. Cannaday had wanted it, and so there could be seen the three metal prongs on the back, one at each side, halfway up, and one at the bottom. They worked easily enough, but twice the leatherette backing slipped down, until Miss Ferguson took over again, gritting her teeth painfully, and at last managed the thing. And after that there was no urgency at all, not from then on—a slow, trancelike quality of mind, rather. The thing had proved itself out now. No crazy hoping any more, no worries, no fear. The letter was there.

But the right letter?

Before she had any chance to make sure that it was, she heard a car over on Greenway Road behind her. As soon as she heard it, she tried to do too many things in the same instant. She grabbed the letter first, then the snapshot for no sensible reason, she turned off the lamp, and she spun hurriedly about in order to face the three big windows in front. She spun a little too hurriedly. She knocked the picture frame from the bedside table and stepped on it. Glass crunched. She stood in pitch blackness once more.

And she had no idea of what to do after that. She ran over to the middle window, bumping into the fireplace chair on the way, and then stood there, still holding the letter and the snapshot in her right hand, until the car outside had droned steadily on toward the state highway. After that she whispered to herself, closed her eyes for another moment and groped for the reading lamp that must be just beside her on the French writing desk.

Then it was possible to see the postmark on the letter, a Poughkeepsie postmark. Inside, in neat, classical script, were three handwritten pages. The last one had been signed by William J. Bennett, M.D., in a different and obviously shaky handwriting. There were two other signatures to the left of that, and under it. One was the Reverend Joseph J. Carroll, O.S.F. The other was that of Brother Michael Francis.

But now the light had begun dazzling her. She snapped it off. It seemed that she was a little afraid of it, with no warning; it was the darkness that had become warm and friendly to her, and that offered protection. A second car came along Greenway Road, but she was Miss Ferguson in full truth now, and so she retained crisp command over herself. She knew exactly what she had to do. She had to make sure of the letter, she had to leave everything else as she had found it in this bedroom, she had to lock the door as she went out, and then she had to return Mrs. Bradley's key ring. In two or three minutes after that, she would be back at the car; in five more, back in Lucy's room at the Cortlandt Arms, mission accomplished. So . . .

But the darkness was not quite so dark as before, oddly. Why? Then she saw why. A delicate pale tracery of light was circling around through the closed bedroom drapes one after another. But Miss Ferguson found herself not even faintly disturbed by that development. Why should she be? A friend calling, someone who wanted to express polite regret about Mrs. Cannaday—and so nothing to worry about. Let them ring at the front door; let them wake Paddy if they wanted to. It would be still all right. Paddy had no key to the house. The thing to do,

162

then, was to wait quietly in this room until whoever it was had driven off again, and for Miss Ferguson to part the drapes just a little for herself, and look down at the car. What was she worried about?

So she parted the drapes, and looked down, and it was a very familiar car—a big gray Cadillac convertible. It pulled up now in the gravel turnaround under the windows, and the door opened over on the driver's side. Robert Burden got out. A moment later, coming around into the headlights, little Elizabeth joined him. He handed her his keys, pointed up at the house and said something. She skipped away, out of vision from the second-floor bedroom. The terrace lights were turned on. The car lights were turned off. He followed Elizabeth.

Now a faintly reflected illumination came up from the terrace, whitening the draperies. It was not full light, but enough—even if that odd, trancelike quality of mind was becoming a bit bothersome again—to lead Miss Ferguson out into the hall without mishap. There she closed the door very quietly after her, and locked it quietly. Then—for there was a switch at the foot of the hall stairs—all the corridor lights flashed on over her. He was coming up.

"All right," Miss Ferguson warned her at that development. "Steady on now. Just don't panic. You've got all the time in the world yet. You locked the door, didn't you? Good. Now you've got to slip back to the service stairs, but the door to it is a swing door, remember, so don't let it swing out into the hall behind you. He might notice that. Just ease it back into place after us. That's it. Now wait a moment. We're still perfectly safe, I tell you. Just wait until he goes into his room, which he will, probably, and until you know where the child is, and then we'll slip down the service stairs before he knows we're anywhere around in here, and get out through the kitchen and the back door. There's

163

nothing at all to get excited about, not if you still have the letter, anyway. And you do, of course. You weren't silly enough to . . . No, don't think you have it. Make sure, nitwit. It's the only way to settle the thing. You have, haven't you?"

And of course she did. Yes. Funny thing, however. She was carrying it in her left hand, although she remembered having picked it up with her right in Mrs. Cannaday's bedroom. And it felt rather big and thick for a letter—glossy, oversized. So she turned her head slowly, to make quite sure, as directed, and in the one narrow beam of light that slanted through at her from the edge of the swing door saw what she was holding now in her left hand. It should have been the letter. It had to be! But it was not. It was little Elizabeth's snapshot.

She remained quite still, turned to it, looking at it. Perhaps ten seconds went past. Then she could hear his voice out there, and his footsteps. He entered his room. But would he stay in there? It seemed to Miss Ferguson that she knew better than that, and knew instantly. No. There could be only one reason why he had got rid of the servants today, and come back here alone with the child at this hour. He intended to search Mrs. Cannaday's bedroom again, and this time with perfect and assured privacy for himself. Although search was not the correct word for it, not now. If Miss Ferguson had grabbed up the snapshot a minute ago, then she must have left the letter on that writing desk—and so it would probably be the first thing he noticed when he entered Mrs. Cannaday's bedroom.

She made her first movement then—a sudden and distracted gesture of her right hand against the wall behind her. To be that stupid! To have had the letter, and then to . . . She repeated the movement, even more distractedly. Or was there still a chance for her, even now?

164

He might remain in his room for five or ten minutes. He might send Elizabeth off to bed before he did anything. Was there a chance, then?

She considered the possibility. It seemed to her that she considered it calmly and coolly, from Miss Ferguson's angle. And what was necessary, after all? Just to slip back into Mrs. Cannaday's room, to get the letter and to slip out again before he heard anything. Very simple, the simplest thing in the world, perhaps—unless he heard her. And then . . .

She was very stupid once more. She was aware of a low, anguished noise in the throat, turning her head from the corridor. No, she understood, no, she couldn't. She had done enough now, but the silly emotional one had spoiled everything. So she couldn't. She had used up every possible reserve in her. It might be that she could force herself to open the swing door a bare inch, in order to see what the child was doing, and whether or not the second-floor corridor was still empty. But to even attempt anything else . . .

She edged open the swing door. After that she could see part of the hall down from her: the light green carpet, the landing, the grandfather's clock, the door to Robert Burden's bedroom standing wide open. Was he still in there? He was. He placed himself. One of his windows was thrown up, and then the other one. Yes, Miss Ferguson thought, with a feeling of rather fantastic serenity taking over in her. Very hot in the house; and then, of course, the windows had been closed for three or four hours now, and so Robert Burden desired coolness and fresh air for himself. Why not? Miss Ferguson desired those things, too. There was not so much as a breath of coolness in the service passage. Even more, however, at just this moment, she desired a little time in which she could reflect on a suitable course of action for herself. She could never force herself out into the corridor again, into plain sight for him. The thing was impossible. And yet if she didn't . . .

He moved in there, just five or six steps, and sat down on the bed. She heard it creak under him—and it would creak again, the thought came to her, when he got up. So there would be at least that small help, the next time he moved—an alarm bell at the right instant. Would it be warning enough?

She had no idea. She tried not to think about it too much. Twice, bodily forcing herself, she started out into the corridor, trying desperately not to consider the chances and probabilities any more, but to act, rather; and twice, unable to stop herself, she crouched back again into the darkness and safety of the service passage. The third time, although bothered by a nightmare idea that she was moving much more slowly and noisily than she wanted to move, she made the plunge. She moved out into the hall, halfway between his bedroom and Mrs. Cannaday's. She crossed the hall. She even got the door unlocked. But then, keeping her head turned to the next room down, to his room, so that she could watch and listen for the first movement in there with agonizing intensity, she did something that she should never have done.

She dropped the key ring.

And he heard it. He got up at once, as Miss Ferguson bent blindly, and snatched blindly, and then he came out into the hall no more than a second after she got into Mrs. Cannaday's room and closed the door behind her and locked it on the simple turn catch from the inside. She could not see him after that, but she could hear him. He moved away toward the main stairs.

"Libby?" he called out. "What was that? What are you doing in there?"

The child answered him from her room, over on the other side of the landing. Miss Ferguson could hear the voice faintly, not the words.

"Well, you did," he insisted now. "Something dropped out here. I heard it. But what did you do with my keys? I gave them to you down at the car, didn't I?"

Keys, Miss Ferguson thought, still crouched—and one of them, without question, the key to Mrs. Cannaday's room. The child answered faintly again. He lost patience.

"I mean when I told you to open the front door and put on the lights," he said. "That's when. Now go down and get them for me. You must have left them right there on the hall table."

Which meant another reprieve for Miss Ferguson, though a very brief one. She did her best with it. The terrace light was still on downstairs, and the window end of the room was not quite so black as the corridor end. But she could see no letter on the writing desk, and none on the rug under it. Where, then? The bedside table? She turned quickly in that direction, and felt something or other in the slash pocket of her summer skirt, something that crinkled up against her. And she knew what it was, she knew even before she put her hand into the pocket, and felt it. It was the letter, and she had been carrying it in there the whole time. Miss Ferguson had made another little mistake.

She whispered something or other. Physically weak then, she had to rest her head against the hall door for a moment. And now what? He was still out there on the landing, moving about audibly. Should she try to call someone from the phone on the bedside table? Should she attempt to get a little outside help for herself? She turned toward it, groping with both hands—and then froze again. No. It was proving to be turnabout indeed, now. It was a dial phone, and even out in the hall he would hear her dialing on it. Why not? She could hear him, couldn't she?

Then she remembered the other phone, the one on

167

the wall—the house phone. Paddy? She reached for that, and discovered that it would not be so simple there, either. She remembered that there were four red buttons under the box, but she could not remember which of them was the cottage connection. She very nearly pressed all of them, in blind panic, before it came to her that if she did that the one in the kitchen would ring, and the one in Mrs. Bradley's bedroom, which meant that he would be warned instantly. So Miss Ferguson realized that she would have to risk a light again, for just a second or two; no other way out of it. Was there time?

She risked it, in any event—and the button she wanted was the fourth button. "Cottage," it said, in neat typing, and she pressed it. And she got the cottage right away. The bell began ringing at the other end. She heard it. But at the same moment she heard something else. She heard the child coming upstairs, and that man speaking to her. After that, consequently, Miss Ferguson could only lay the phone part up on the box, in order that the bell would keep ringing and ringing now. Then she switched off the bedside lamp, and started around the bed itself for the big walk-in closet just opposite her.

But the closet could offer no protection. She realized before she got halfway across to it that he had searched there last night, but in only a quick, sketchy manner, and so he must intend to search there again tonight, and much more thoroughly this time. The bathroom, perhaps? She reversed direction, starting back for the bathroom, but at once the same objection presented itself. Then where?

And now keys were rattling on the other side of the hall door, and there was no time at all for Miss Ferguson to stand frozen stupidly in position before it, while she debated the merits of various hiding places. He was

168

coming in now. She had about two or three seconds. She retreated hurriedly, nothing sensible coming to her, found herself back beside the writing desk, and squeezed in there, at the middle window of the room, behind the floor-length white draperies. A moment afterward the door was pushed open, and the ceiling light turned on from the switch beside it.

He came in.

She could see him quite clearly then, though without wanting to see him. The window drapes were of some thick, silky material, but with thin slits visible when close up—and Miss Ferguson, with the corner of the window behind her, had to stand very close up. The effect, therefore, was of a pane of one-way glass between them, he fully revealed from behind the draperies, but, from his distance, Miss Ferguson not revealed to him. He glanced from side to side first, and then back quickly at something else that had been forgotten. It was the picture frame. It was still lying where Miss Ferguson had dropped it minutes ago by the bedside table.

Broken glass twinkled up at him from the white carpet. He stared down at it, head turned awkwardly over his right shoulder. Then he bent, picking up the frame in one of his hands and the leatherette backing in the other. Miss Ferguson could not see his expression at that moment, but it was not necessary to see it. In there, Robert Burden must have been telling himself—in there, where any half-witted fool should have known that it was. In there!

He straightened, still with his back to her, and walked over to the hall door.

"Libby!" he called out. His voice, deep as ever, appeared a bit strained and effortful to Miss Ferguson; but perhaps, with only the child to manage now, it did not seem to him that he would have to be as careful as usual. "Come here," he said. "Come here, Libby."

She came. A small, sleepily petulant face was presented to him from the hall doorway, a ribbon in the brown hair, and a big picture book tucked in under the right arm.

"I was just going to bed," Elizabeth Burden complained fretfully. "And I got you the keys, didn't I? What do you want?"

He might have given her that slow, oddly vague smile of his, to ease matters; Miss Ferguson had the impression that he did so, at any rate. He was still holding the frame in one hand and the backing in the other, holding them out to Elizabeth. And now he was only a few feet distant from the house phone beside Mrs. Cannaday's bed, so that he might easily have heard the faint ringing at the other end of it. He did not, however. The frame absorbed him. He looked at Elizabeth, at the frame and then back to Elizabeth again.

"I know you're tired," he said. "We both are. It's been a long day, hasn't it? And that's why I decided that we'd better fly down to Virginia tomorrow morning, Libby. I thought you should get a good night's sleep for yourself. That's why we came back here."

It was fatherly consideration from him, but, quite patently, altogether unaccustomed consideration. The line of defense was up against it. The child shrugged coolly.

"Well, I wish we hadn't," she told him. "I don't like it without anyone here. And you told Paddy that we were going to drive down to Virginia, too, after we had dinner in Rhinebeck. I heard you."

"I know," he repeated, with patient gentleness again, or the pretense of it. But why? Miss Ferguson began asking herself. What did he want? How could the child help him? "Only then," he said, "we'd have had to keep driving all night. I thought it might be just a little too much for you, Libby."

Or too much for him, Miss Ferguson realized—with the letter still in this room somewhere. He was a cold-blooded and cautious man. He put first things first. And so he had rid himself of the servants this afternoon, they driving in one car, he and Libby following in another. Only he had not followed. He had, rather, managed the whole thing so that no one at all could bother him to-night, so that he could examine this bedroom inch by inch, if need be. Yet his action would appear to be deep and proper concern for the child. Who could object to it? He was not even half a fool. At all points he was still carefully protecting himself.

He held up the picture frame.

"But who broke this?" he asked her. "And who took your picture out of it? Did you, Libby? Tell me the truth, please. I won't be angry with you. I promise. I just want to know about it, that's all."

Yes, Miss Ferguson told herself; that was all. That explained all this unusual gentleness in him. He did want to know about it. He wanted to know very much.

"That old thing?" Elizabeth said. She shrugged again, still indifferent. "I wasn't even upstairs," she said. "Miss Thornton wouldn't let me come up." Then she smiled secretly and maliciously to herself, as if well satisfied about something, and glanced up at him from her eye corners. "But I saw those men, anyway," she said. "And I know what they were doing up here. Ha-ha. They carried Grandmother away in a big box, didn't they?"

He sat down on the bed, in profile to Miss Ferguson, and very dangerously close now to the house telephone. Close enough to hear the ringing from it, or a sleepy and puzzled murmur from Paddy the groom at the other end? Apparently not. The picture frame was what mat-tered now to Robert Burden. He held it up again, the fatherly smile getting a bit strained, perhaps, but still trying to achieve the closest possible sympathy and un-

171

derstanding about this business between father and daughter. Only that was a new experience for him. He had never bothered with it before. He had to push for what he wanted, and the child knew it. There was still that bright-eyed small malice in her. She was getting her own back.

"Maybe I did break it," she said. "I don't know. Maybe I broke it last week sometime."

He wet his lips delicately, watching her, attempting to read her.

"Please," he said. "Please, Libby. Don't fool about this. If you broke it sometime today, then I won't mind. It's perfectly all right. But you see I locked everything up in here early this morning, and so I can't understand how you got in, or how anybody else could. That's what worries me. Whoever it was might have stolen something."

And that was a very dramatic suggestion, indeed. It woke up Elizabeth. She smiled secretly again, delighted with the idea, and beginning to swing herself on one foot in the hall doorway.

"Then I know who it was," she said, nodding at him, very sure of herself now, very adult. "It was some of those men. They did it."

"No," he said. "No, it wasn't, Libby. Your picture was right here on the bedside table this morning. I saw it. But Mrs. Bradley has a key to this room, too. Perhaps someone got it from her this afternoon, and came in here. So think a minute. This is very important to me."

And it was, Miss Ferguson understood. What had happened? Elizabeth hopped over to the big fireplace chair, sat down very low in it, with both her legs thrust out, and dropped the picture book.

"Maybe it just fell," she suggested. "Maybe the wind blew it."

He made a quick, angry motion, still not sure of the

172

child, still studying her, and got up abruptly in order to conceal that he had.

"No, it didn't," he said. "It couldn't have. The windows in here were closed all day, Libby, and they're still closed. So who took that snapshot? Somebody must have. Did you see Miss Ferguson up here at all? She could have asked Mrs. Bradley for the key this morning. Perhaps she forgot something. I want you to think, Libby."

It was becoming breathlessly hot in back of the draperies. The room light shone through with a thick, muzzy effect, and Miss Ferguson's eyes were aching and stinging against it. Her back ached, too, with the window edge pressing in more and more on her, but after that remark from Mr. Robert Burden she did not permit herself to move so much as a finger.

So, uneasy after last night, he did have at least a few suspicions about Miss Ferguson—which meant that if she were discovered now, and with the letter on her, she could be presumed to know everything, as Katie Stoner had known everything. And what had happened to Katie Stoner? Yet it was at least a small gift of Providence that he was still talking to the child in this way. It prevented him from hearing anything at all from the house phone. But had Paddy heard anything yet, or would he hear it? That was even more important. So Miss Ferguson began to pray silently that Paddy would hear it, and that, just by way of a very tiny miracle, the child would be permitted to go back to her room now, and to remain there, whatever else happened. After that it could end between them however it had to end, between Miss Ferguson and that man. But the child . . .

"Who?" Elizabeth said. Now she was altogether slouched in the fireplace chair, chin and stomach on the same level, and had begun to swing the tips of her shoes together. She was much too interested in doing that very slowly and carefully to pay proper attention to him; but

173

then what he wanted from her—wholehearted concern for his problem, willing sympathy and thoughtfulness about it—he had never wanted before. Her thoughts wandered from the subject at hand. She was bored by it, and by him. And again, most beautifully this time, it was his training.

"I liked Miss Ferguson," she said, the small brown head sinking lower and lower, the shoe tips once more touching each other. "I liked her almost as much as Miss Proctor. She was nice."

No use, he must have realized then; and as a direct result of that, no more need for patience and gentleness. It must have been pretty much of a strain on him by this time. But now the natural man could shine through, the contempt and dislike could be revealed to her. They were revealed.

"And you liked Miss Chisholm," he said, the crisp English mustache curling sarcastically. "She was pretty. You like everybody, don't you? Papa's little charmer. I wonder if they like you, however. That's the question."

"Well, they did," Elizabeth said, again with that maddening shrill laugh of hers, to irritate and defy him in her usual manner. "Ha-ha. They said so. They all said so. And I could tell, anyway."

He might have permitted her that one small comfort. He did not. It seemed that he could not leave her alone, even now. There must have been long habit in him. Detach her from everyone in the world, from even the most normal and ordinary contact with other people, crush ruthlessly any childlike groping in that direction— and then he would have her. There would be nothing to worry Robert Burden after that. It would be his wish for her, his will and his command. Now he looked down at the very small figure in the fireplace chair, and smiled gently.

"Then I wonder why they used to refer to you as the

little horror," he said. "And I heard them. But you don't seem able to tell about that, do you?"

She was very low in the chair. She got lower, so that Miss Ferguson could not see whatever expression she had now. But that was all right. Miss Ferguson did not want to see it. She had turned her head away in back of the draperies. Her two hands had clenched.

"Well, I don't care," Elizabeth said. There was a pause. "I don't care," she repeated breathlessly. "They didn't have to like me. I didn't like them, either. I just said that I did. Ha-ha."

"How very clever that is," he remarked ironically, and perhaps while still smiling at her. "How very brilliant. You didn't like them, either. Well, remember it next time. Remember who you are, and who they are. Or try, anyway. Now get to bed."

Hatred, Miss Ferguson found it necessary to warn herself at that point, was not a civilized emotion, nor in these circumstances a useful or desirable one; and yet there obviously were occasions when civilized people could feel it shaking in them, and shaking very nearly out of control, too. When she was able to again look out from the draperies, forcing herself, Elizabeth was walking away from her toward the hall door, feet dragging a bit, small head down. The picture book was forgotten. It was still lying on the floor beside the fireplace chair. Of course, Miss Ferguson had to realize. Other considerations now. A little horror . . . The child did not say anything else after that. He didn't. She went out.

So it was between them now, Miss Ferguson understood, and it would end between them. She felt quite ready. Again, as on another occasion a few days ago, she never wavered a bit from then on. She waited and watched. He closed the hall door after Elizabeth, took off his jacket, threw it over viciously onto Mrs. Cannaday's bed and began with the bookcase.

And now it was much different for him than last night. There was no hurry at all, and so Robert Burden did not hurry. He was slow, thorough and methodical. At the bookcase he removed the books one by one, shook them out and inspected the shelves afterward. Then he removed all the magazines from the rack, and riffled them. The heavy face had begun to look tighter and uglier than usual. He was sweating a bit.

He went into the bathroom, but there was just the linen closet in there, and the medicine cabinet. He came out of the bathroom. When he did, with his collar unbuttoned and his tie loose, the perspiration was even more noticeable on him. He took a handkerchief out of his pocket and wiped his cheeks with it, then under his chin. After that he decided to do a very natural thing. He decided to open up the windows.

But he gave no warning to Miss Ferguson about that decision, not even the least warning. He might have begun with the end window on her right, or the other end window over on her left, but he had the luck of the devil again. He began with her window, and of course finished with it. Before she had any idea of what he intended to do, he walked straight ahead toward her, flung the drapes back one to each side, and so was standing directly in front of Miss Ferguson, arms up and out, before she realized that she would have no protection at all from now on.

She did manage to twist herself down and to one side under his right arm. She even managed to get four or five steps over toward the hall door—no further, however. By the time she had reached the bookcase, he succeeded in flinging himself around after her, and catching her skirt. She tore loose, after struggling desperately against him, and broke away. Then he took no chances at all. He got hold of her once more, spun her around to him and then hit her.

176

It was never clear to Miss Ferguson how often he hit her, nor even where, for that matter. It was just that things spun blindly, the floor sweeping up under her, the light spinning into darkness, and then into light again. She felt no pain, but only a confused, jarring sensation of physical shock. Yet a moment afterward she seemed to be quite normal once more, although not quite settled in her accustomed manner of thought and of bodily movement. But he had stopped hitting her. He seemed to have vanished suddenly. Why? Tony? She was all alone in the room.

Using both her hands, she succeeded in dragging herself up against the fireplace chair, and discovered then that she was not so very much alone, after all. He was over by the hall door, and again facing her. She could see his lips move, but it was not possible to understand what he was saying to her. Then all at once her ears must have popped out, as she was still crouched, because she could hear his voice in the room, and under it and surrounding it a low, scratchy rumbling, like that of a cheap phonograph record before the music comes on.

". . . never wanted anything like this," Robert Burden was telling her, a grimace as of faint gentlemanly distaste on his lips. "But I'm afraid you rather surprised me, Miss Ferguson. I didn't realize who you were for the moment. But how did you get into this room tonight? What did you want in here?"

She did not deny anything. She did not even think of the one feeble excuse that Paddy had let her in, that Paddy knew she was here. She permitted the hatred to lead her on against him, and before thinking.

"What you wanted," she said. "What you were looking for last night, Mr. Burden. Or don't you remember?"

"Oh, yes," he said. It was still hot in the room. He had not opened the windows a moment ago, but now, for him as for Miss Ferguson, the heat was no longer important in any way. "I remember," he said. "When you were out there in the hall spying on me. I couldn't understand why you were, however. I still don't."

Any minute, she tried comforting herself—Tony. Then draw it out with him for as long as she could, because Tony was the one hope for her, and for the letter. Paddy must not have heard the phone ringing and ringing over there in his cottage, and so Paddy would never hear a cry over there, either. Of course, too, there would be only one cry permitted. Mr. Robert Burden did not have to put that thought into crude words for her. It was the first tacit agreement between them. And who else was here at Ridge Hill tonight? The child, of course, over there on the other side of the corridor landing. Did she want to involve the child, however? He was almost at the end of his string now, and perhaps desperate enough to do whatever would have to be done to Miss Ferguson. What mattered, then, was that he must not be made desperate enough to think of doing it to the child, also. She got to her knees.

"That's right," she said. "You still don't. Then it's a very simple matter, Mr. Burden. I've spied on you. I've broken and entered. You call the police."

"In good time," he nodded, still planted calmly and solidly in front of the hall door. "Don't worry about it. And don't try to push me, Miss Ferguson. I wouldn't advise it. What did you want in this room?"

She had put her hand down on the outside of her slash pocket, to make sure about the letter. It was still there. Now she removed the hand, in order that the pocket would not become noticeable and significant to him.

"And I'd advise you," she said, still supporting herself on both knees over at the fireplace chair. "Don't try any games with me, Mr. Burden. I have friends at the hotel, and I left word for them. They'll be here any minute."

"Well, of course," he said, again mopping calmly under his shirt collar, and around his mouth. "Yes. Any minute at all. I expected that. Friends and reinforcements; the local fire brigade. But I asked you two questions, Miss Ferguson. What were you doing in this room tonight? What did you want?"

She understood then that she had been handling him in the wrong way, and that it might be just a little too late to begin handling him in the right way. She made the attempt, however. She began to cry.

"Ask Paddy," she heard herself sob brokenly. "You hurt my arm. I forgot my fountain pen, that's all. And Paddy let me in to—"

"No, please," Robert Burden said. With his right hand he made a charmingly courteous gesture, in appeal for a little common sense and common honesty between them. "That's why you hid from me in this room, and watched me last night from out in the hall? Let's try it again, Miss Ferguson. Paddy couldn't have let you in. He had no key. And a fountain pen— Now, really, Miss Ferguson. What did you want here?"

"I've told you," she said. "Ask Paddy."

He considered her, hands behind him, dull eyes narrowed.

"Don't do that," he said quietly. "Not tonight, Miss Ferguson. I'm not in the mood."

And then the hatred betrayed her even more recklessly. She pushed herself up from the fireplace chair.

"No," she said. "You're not in the mood, not after Katie Stoner and Rocky Point, Mr. Burden. That's true enough."

He stirred slightly at that, but just slightly.

"Why, that's absurd," he said, and repeated that negligently charming gesture of a moment ago, to prove that it was. "I don't even know what it's intended to mean, Miss Ferguson. Do you?"

And she had to bait him after that question, as he had

baited a seven-year-old child minutes ago. There was no resisting the opportunity he had presented to her.

"How very clever that is," she remarked scornfully. "How very brilliant, Mr. Burden. You don't even know what it's intended to mean. Well, Miss Ferguson doesn't know, either. How could she? But would you suppose that the child's mother might know? Is that any sort of a reasonable possibility to you?"

He gave that very slight flicker of the lips again, as he had out in the corridor earlier this morning with Dr. McCormick. But they were quite alone now, and he did not bother to conceal it by using the handkerchief. He only nodded calmly, still resting himself against the bedroom door with that at-ease slouchiness of his, while studying her face feature by feature. Then he nodded a second time. He did not deny anything, either. They were past that.

"So that's it," he said. "The child's mother—and in this house. I see. You know I've sometimes wondered about you. The type of woman, I mean. Two or three hundred dollars from someone like Katie Stoner, and glad to be rid of the little bastard once and for all, with no questions asked. But do forgive me, Miss Ferguson. I'm employing the term in a quite literal fashion, you understand. Sorry. And of course that's another story, isn't it? Seven years ago. Well, what's the new price, Miss Ferguson? Or haven't you decided yet with all those green fields of clover ahead?"

And the hatred lay between them now. It was a naked force in the room, as much on his side as on hers. It was only that there were rather different reasons for it.

"You haven't enough." Miss Ferguson whispered back at him, her voice shaking a bit here, for the first time. "And you never will have enough! Not for what you've done to her, or tried to do. I thought she was

180

dead. They lied to me. But if you think— Oh, no, Mr. Burden. Not again!"

"So they told you it was dead," Robert Burden observed, beginning to push himself out step by step from the hall door, without ever taking his brown eyes from her. "Of course. Some kind friend, to spare your feelings. But either way it was still a relief to you, wasn't it? I imagine the resemblance struck you at the hospital that time. Then the same town, of course. Then the same birth date, even, once you managed to start up a conversation with her. Was that it?"

He came forward another few steps, slowly and deliberately. Behind him, when he had just about reached the foot of Mrs. Cannaday's bed, the hall door opened.

"I forgot my picture book," Elizabeth complained fretfully. "And I want it. Who are you talking to?"

Then she saw Miss Ferguson standing back of the fireplace chair, and paused briefly. He did not. He was very quick then. He got back of Elizabeth, between her and the hall door, and dropped a hand on each of the small shoulders, while another complete understanding flashed back and forth between him and Miss Ferguson. She could appeal for help now, to the child. It was her choice. But if she did . . .

"Hi," Elizabeth said, and blinked sleepily. "I didn't hear you come upstairs. Did you ring? I thought . . ."

At that point she must have remembered the little horror. Miss Ferguson could see it in her. The small face hardened. The small body drew itself up stiff as a flagpole.

"Where's my picture book?" she demanded imperiously. "Where did I leave it?"

"Over there," Robert Burden said, edging her on a little to the fireplace chair, but still watching Miss Ferguson. "On the floor, Libby. And Miss Ferguson came back to get her fountain pen. She saw our lights on. That's all."

"I wouldn't care what she forgot," Elizabeth said, speaking in a high, clear tone, and with her chin up. "It doesn't matter to me. Why should it? I want my picture book."

She twitched away from him, her eyes flashing, and Miss Ferguson bent down for the picture book. It was a very natural action on her part, everything considered, or she hoped that it was. But then the picture book appeared too big for her to manage with one hand. She dropped it. She dropped it back of the magazine rack, and then had to turn slightly in order to pick it up again. That gave her three or four seconds when she had the right side of her body hidden from him—just long enough, without delaying obviously, to get the letter out of her skirt pocket and slip it in between the first two pages of the picture book.

"Here," Miss Ferguson said, and with the most extraordinary evenness and precision of tone, it seemed to her. Had he noticed anything? It seemed not. Yet he was still careful enough to remain in back of the child, in guard position between her and the hall door.

"Here it is," Miss Ferguson said. "Is this what you want?"

"Thank you," Elizabeth said, cool, stiffly erect, even more imperious. "How very kind you are. Yes, it is."

And that satisfied him. He stood aside from the hall door, but still in guard position.

"Then all right," he said. "Get over to bed, Libby. Miss Ferguson was just leaving."

But she had always shown Robert Burden, and now it became necessary for her to show Miss Ferguson also. She uttered that shrill, penetrating child's laugh, and slapped the picture book against her right leg to express fitting nonchalance. The second time she did that, when she was in the second-floor corridor once more, the letter dropped out.

Miss Ferguson saw it drop out. She was facing in that direction. He did not. Still watching Miss Ferguson, he reached over with his left hand and closed the door after Elizabeth. But the last minute or two might have produced a certain strain in him, too. He used the handkerchief again, the tanned square face glistening.

"I believe that was wise of you," he remarked. "Good sense. But then she really couldn't have helped very much, could she?"

"No, she couldn't," Miss Ferguson said. Tony . . . Tony! "I wasn't too much aware that she had to, for that matter. Now I'd advise you to open that door, Mr. Burden. I'm not frightened."

"When she's over in her room," he said, very calm again. "In just a moment. Where's the letter?"

She had admitted everything else to him out of her blind hatred. She admitted the letter now, at last recklessly triumphant against him.

She laughed aloud.

"Not back of the snapshot," she said. "Not any more, Mr. Burden. Too bad, isn't it?"

"Well, yes," he agreed, speaking softly and carefully now, moistening the lips. "I'm afraid it is. And more for you than for me, Miss Ferguson, in that case. You won't tell me?"

"How very brilliant," she said, still keeping the fireplace chair between them. "No. I won't tell you. Never in this world, Mr. Burden. It's out of your hands."

The smile got a bit slower and vaguer than she remembered it, the lips were moistened a second time, rather delicately.

"I warn you," he said. "You're giving me no choice, Miss Ferguson. Where is it?"

"Now let me see," she said, still openly mocking him, to have him forget the child at this moment, and to be altogether concentrated on Miss Ferguson. "It's around somewhere. It would have to be, wouldn't it, Mr. Burden? We could try under the rug, after you're through searching me, of course, or back of the radiator over there. But let me think a minute. What did I do with it?"

He came forward another step, lips parted a bit, flat cheeks glistening, and spun off the fireplace chair between them. It went over. He paid no attention to it.

"All right," she said, her voice shaking again, with all the physical dread she still felt of the man, of the touch of his hand on her, making Miss Ferguson properly and convincingly desperate against him. Where was Tony? What was keeping him all this time? "Just stay away," she said. "Don't threaten me, Mr. Burden. I heard you when you came in—and I dropped it out of the window over there. Go down and look."

He wiped his mouth in a rough, savage manner with his right hand, an unexpected animal gesture in Mr. Robert Burden, glanced over at the window behind them, glanced back at her.

"I'll look with you," he said. "With you, Miss Ferguson. Come on."

And the door opened again; Elizabeth again. She was holding the letter in both hands, and looking at it. He spun around to the door. Who? he must have asked himself. The brat again?

"Now I told you—" he shouted furiously.

Then he saw the letter, and stopped shouting. Before he could move for it, however, Miss Ferguson threw herself forward and knocked him back across one leg of the fireplace chair. It caught him off balance. He went down, shouting again, and striking back passionately at her.

And the child saw that. She saw his face, mottled and blood-dark in spots, she saw the expression on it, and she saw him strike again and again, completely maddened

184

by this time, even when he had Miss Ferguson on the floor under him. It must have been something that the child had suspected often before in him, a thing there, a savage and hidden physical violence, but now she had it fully revealed to her. She became terrified, backing out into the hall from him, and shaking her head blindly. He saw that. He tried to change.

"Libby," he said, wheedling fatuously with one hand out, and the other supporting him beside the fireplace chair. "Don't be frightened. That's Grandmother's letter, isn't it? Give it to me. That's what I wanted. Give me the letter, Libby. It's all right."

But very probably Elizabeth had forgotten the letter. She backed off another step, still holding it. Then she ran.

And when she did, when he started after her, scrambling up madly on hands and knees, Miss Ferguson again threw the fireplace chair over on him, and pinned him down. She had been hit on the left side or the left shoulder, but not importantly. She managed the thing. He was an extremely powerful man, however. He got up despite her, reached the door and plunged out drunkenly. When she had followed him out, weeping now, and dragging herself hand by hand on the white rug, he was all the way down to the corridor landing, and struggling with Paddy.

"Now, sir," Paddy was saying, all anxious and bewildered. "Now, Mr. Burden, sir—"

He was not deliberately in the way, but he was in the way, nevertheless. He was flung bodily into the stair railing, came off it, and grabbed a second time at Mr. Burden, to save himself. They toppled together down the main stairway, all the way down. One of them got up at the bottom of it. The other one lay quite motionless, dull little brown eyes glaring back, unwinking and wide open, mouth distorted.

185

So then there was indeed a broken and crumpled body lying down there beside the big stair post at Ridge Hill, but it was not Miss Ferguson's body, after all. She turned helplessly from it, the back of one hand over her mouth, and saw Elizabeth, silent and stricken, crouched back from her on the far side of the big grandfather's clock. A bit later, when Miss Ferguson was on her knees over there, whispering whatever she could think of to whisper. Paddy came up from the lower hall. He was still bewildered.

"But I heard the phone," he babbled out foolishly, to excuse himself. "It woke me up, miss—and then all I could hear on it was some kind of crazy commotion, like. So I came over to see was there anything wrong in the house, and the front door wasn't locked, and I came in to see whether . . ." He stopped, facing back to the stairs, and made another befuddled motion with his right arm. "Good God," he said. "Good God, miss. He's still lying down there. I think he's broken his neck."

"I know," Miss Ferguson said, cradling a small brown head against her, and again closing her eyes helplessly. "I saw him. Get a blanket or something. Please, Paddy. Just cover his face, would you? Then call Dr. McCormick."

¶TWELVE

So for Miss Ferguson there was only one more afternoon at Ridge Hill after that, but a rather long afternoon, and several days later. Other people were with her that time. There was Dr. Quinlan, first of all, who had driven her up, and Lucy's friend Max Benzinger, and another man, tall, portly and precise, with a magnificent mane of gray hair and distinguished aquiline features.

He was introduced to Miss Ferguson as Mr. Allan Fuller, of Fuller, Hamilton and DeVries.

"Very big law firm," little Max Benzinger explained softly. "Twenty-two senior partners, and thirty or forty junior ones. So let's watch ourselves. We're in very fast company, Miss Ferguson."

"Why, thank you," Mr. Fuller said, beaming down at him with an expression of fierce relish. "That's appreciated from you, Max. But where's the goatee and the corncob pipe? You're up in the country, aren't you?"

"Such talk," Max Benzinger said, shaking his head sadly at Miss Ferguson from the other side of the library table. "When my learned colleague knows that the law is an exercise in pure logic—for lawyers, anyway. But let's see what we have for him. You'd better sit down, Allie. You're on the wrong side of the gate this time, and I think you know it."

"We'll find out," Mr. Fuller said grimly. "In due course. But come on. Just what do you think you have for me? Let's see it."

They began to confer. The big, booming voice, confident and self-assured, from Allan Fuller; the shy, hesitant little one, patient as time, from Max Benzinger. A letter was produced, the letter. Allan Fuller read it with evident amusement, chuckled aloud two or three times and then tossed it aside grandly.

"Now, really," Allan Fuller said, as if the letter were quite unworthy of serious consideration between them. "Really, Max. You mean that this is everything that you have for me? You're just wasting my time."

But it was not quite everything. Records from the town hall were introduced—two birth certificates, one death certificate. There followed photostatic copies from Dr. McCormick's office—the blood type of the late Mrs. Robert Burden, which still happened to be on file there, the blood type of the late Mr. Robert Burden, and the blood type, officially certified only the preceding afternoon, of Miss Elizabeth Burden.

"So you see . . ." little Max Benzinger murmured, diffident and apologetic about it. "And here we are with

188

Miss Ferguson's. One way it fits, you understand, and one way it doesn't. It's too bad, Allie. I know how you feel about those nice, fat executor's fees. But I'm afraid that in this case—"

"No, no, no," Allan Fuller said, shaking his head earnestly. "It's not that, Max, and you know it isn't. It's the child. It's a matter of her welfare."

They conferred again. Two people stood outside the library window, within view of Miss Ferguson. One was Dr. Anthony Quinlan, who had a deserved reputation back at the hospital for the way in which he could charm and enchant even very small children. The other wore a yellow ribbon in her brown hair, and swung comfortably back and forth on the terrace railing, listening to him.

"Why?" Allan Fuller boomed. He glanced out of the library window at what he could see of the formal garden, and at the double line of old trees flanking the Ridge Hill driveway. "There," he said, making a fine, sweeping gesture. "That's why. Just think of it. She'll get nothing at all, Max. I hope that's been considered."

"A deathbed confession," little Max Benzinger murmured. "Perfectly acceptable evidence in any court of law in the country, Allie—and you know it. So what's the point of all this?"

The small figure outside lifted its head suddenly to Dr. Quinlan, and laughed aloud, a sound, ringing laugh, and a far better one than Miss Ferguson could remember from her. Nothing? Miss Ferguson thought. She got up, feeling even more sure of herself than Allan Fuller, and crossed over to the library door.

"Oh, yes," Miss Ferguson said. "It's been considered, and it's been decided, too. Thank you very much, Mr. Fuller."

Then she opened the library door, and went out. She was just a little impatient by that time. There were people waiting for her.

83B2706

AN INNER SANCTUM MYSTERY   AN INNER SANCTUM M